To Lois

Enjoy the read!

Lillian Lee Liss

Josefina's Honor

*What Kind of Coin
Will Pay the Piper?*

Lillian Lee Liss

authorHOUSE®

AuthorHouse™
1663 Liberty Drive
Bloomington, IN 47403
www.authorhouse.com
Phone: 1-800-839-8640

© 2011 Lillian Lee Liss. All rights reserved.

No part of this book may be reproduced, stored in a retrieval system, or transmitted by any means without the written permission of the author.

First published by AuthorHouse 8/18/2011

ISBN: 978-1-4567-2793-2 (sc)
ISBN: 978-1-4567-2794-9 (e)

Library of Congress Control Number: 2011901314

Printed in the United States of America

Any people depicted in stock imagery provided by Thinkstock are models, and such images are being used for illustrative purposes only. Certain stock imagery © Thinkstock.

This book is printed on acid-free paper.

Because of the dynamic nature of the Internet, any web addresses or links contained in this book may have changed since publication and may no longer be valid. The views expressed in this work are solely those of the author and do not necessarily reflect the views of the publisher, and the publisher hereby disclaims any responsibility for them.

There's an old saying: "Revenge is a dish best served cold." Sometimes it follows that the aftertaste may be far more bitter than the ingredients in the original recipe.

Chapter 1

Brooklyn – 1947 – The End and the Beginning

It was unusual to have an open coffin at a Jewish funeral. It was open because the distraught mother needed to look at the most beautiful of her six daughters until the last possible moment. Malka Whiteman stood alongside the plain pine coffin, sobbing brokenheartedly while gently patting the silent face. The mournful drone of the organ set the mood in the chapel.

All that could be seen of the dead girl, Gigi Whiteman, was her face, which looked like a wax replica of her former self -- except for the large purple bruise on the chin. Hidden was the lustrous, long black hair, now wrapped in a white cloth. Since the religion demanded that the body must be returned to the earth in the same form in which it entered, the slender body was swathed only in a white shroud. There was no makeup, no fashionable clothing covering the freshly-washed nakedness, no gem on wrist, ear or finger. Yet the classic beauty, the fine outlines of her face could not be hidden. She was only 23 years old, so no wrinkle had yet marred the smooth pale skin, no part of her had had time to age.

One of the funeral parlor attendants took the grieving mother's elbow and led her to a seat. He then closed the casket. A large group had assembled in the funeral chapel. In the first pew sat the dead girl's parents and her five remaining sisters. A confused little boy of about five years old watched his aunts and grandparents crying, so tears began to slide down his little round cheeks too. Other weeping family members sat behind them.

"Where's mommy," he whined, "I want my mommy." His mommy was in the casket and could not come to him. The crying increased and one of his aunts put him on her lap and tried to soothe him. He laid his head on her shoulder and grew quiet.

The murmuring of the mourners in the chapel provided a zephyr of background sound as the rabbi began to intone the Hebrew words of the service. Although he'd never met Gigi, he spoke of the deceased as if he knew her. He told how she was cut down like a sapling, in the full flower of youth. He mentioned her beauty, her talents and the tragedy of her demise. He spoke of a missed future and its possibilities.

Farther back in the chapel a group of four glamorous women, fully made-up as though ready for a party, sat whispering. They had been colleagues of the dead girl, showgirls, they called themselves but really cabaret dancers. They agreed that Gigi had died young and beautiful, that she had lived a full but short, fast and sorry life. No one could have predicted that it would end so soon, so tragically and with such heartbreak, or that the misery generated by her death would go on for years, touching so many of the lives that had touched hers.

Chapter 2

Carroll Gardens, Brooklyn – 26th Precinct

*P*olice Officer Harry O'Hara had been a cop for 29 years. Most of it had been spent patrolling this same neighborhood. He loved his job, especially in the Fall, his favorite time of year. He knew most of the people who lived on his beat, among the brownstone and brick homes of Cobble Hill and Carroll Gardens, the area just above the Brooklyn waterfront. The fine homes here were built to last for the sea captains whose ships brought cargo from the distant corners of the known world to the piers in Brooklyn. Today, the houses, more than a century old, were owned or rented by executives, middle managers, storekeepers and educators, along with the dock workers and old folks who had moved in when the wealthy captains moved out. Most of the children of the previous generation had grown up in the neighborhood and had never left.

The weather this day was special, a typical Indian summer day. Officer O'Hara walked the wide streets and quiet avenues that were canopied by the red- and gold-leafed autumn trees. The delicious food smells coming out of the open windows made saliva gather in the corners of his mouth. He took pleasure in the sounds of children playing on the stoops and sidewalks of the familiar blocks. This was his domain.

In all the years on this beat, the worst things he had ever been called on to resolve or investigate were street fights, auto accidents or domestic squabbles. He knew that many incidents were "settled" within the confines of the home and family, and never reached outside the door. When there were more serious matters, the detectives of the squad were quickly called in and the beat patrol officer's involvement was pretty much finished.

Suddenly, the everyday street noises were shattered by an urgent shout, "Officer, officer, help, hurry, hurry."

The policeman began to run toward a woman standing on a stoop, calling and frantically waving at him. He felt a sense of foreboding at the panic in her voice.

"What's the matter, missus," he asked.

"I tink sometin's wrong," she said, with a strong Italian accent. "You betta come inside and taka da look. I smella da gas," she said in a shaking voice, her forehead wrinkling, while she kept nervously rubbing the side of her face. "Uppa da stairs," she gestured toward the hallway steps leading to the second floor. O'Hara could smell it too, a strong smell of gas.

"Watch out," he yelled, running up the steps. The door to the apartment was locked.

"Do you have the key," he called down. A man lumbered up the stairs, handed him a skeleton key, then ran down. The noxious odor of gas was powerful out in the hallway. After the lock snapped open the officer still had to push hard, bracing his shoulder and legs against the door several times until it gave way. Rags pushed up against the door had made it hard to open. Once inside the gas-filled room he held a handkerchief over his nose and mouth, and with his free hand, he picked up a chair and smashed the window. He turned the knobs on the stove to the off position, opened the other window and waited in the hallway. After several minutes most of the choking odor cleared out. Not until then did he give his attention to the chaos in the room.

Chapter 3

What Happened Here?

He saw a man on a straight-backed kitchen chair, his upper body sprawled across the porcelain-topped table, face down and turned to the side. The man's arms were stretched out in front of him and spittle ran from his mouth. Two other chairs were overturned. A fur coat and a handbag lay on the floor.

On the floor, alongside the table, a woman lay spread-eagled. Her long, jet-black hair fanned out across the patterned, linoleum-covered floor. He couldn't miss the large, purple bruise on her jaw nor the fact that she was very beautiful.

In the doorway four people crowded together to see what was happening. Three men, one who had run upstairs to give the officer the key, and the woman who had called him, stood watching. The officer touched the neck of the man. No pulse. He shook his head. "He's gone." Bending down on one knee, he did the same for the woman.

"I think there's a pulse here," he said excitedly. Since he was looking down at the woman on the floor he didn't notice the sheer panic on the faces of the people at the doorway when he uttered this remark.

Chapter 4

Josefina, Sicily

The streets of the small, sun-baked Sicilian village of Santa Teresa twisted up and around the hillsides into the low mountains that sheltered the hamlet. The town was a few miles inland from Catania, a major city on the coast of Sicily. In midsummer the heart of Santa Teresa, its roads, the houses, even the leaves on the trees seemed dusty and faded to a muddy ochre color. At midday, when the sun was high and hot, the streets were almost empty, giving no hint of the busy life that went on inside the ancient wood-frame, stone and stucco houses. Paint peeled from the aged shutters and doors as well as from the worn signs that advertised the business that went on in each of the shops. The old signs, indicating the wares sold or occupation practiced within the shops were hardly necessary.

Most of the villagers had lived there all their lives and were familiar with what went on in each building -- both publicly and privately. Santa Teresans knew exactly where to find whatever they needed, as well as who was doing what to whom.

Most of the folks who lived there had been born, raised and eventually were laid to their eternal rest within Santa Teresa. They found life good in the little village and few had ventured far beyond. Olive groves, orchards and vineyards dotted the hillsides. These crops thrived in the hot summer sun.

In good years a steady rainfall assured a fine harvest , both to sell and to keep. This provided money for necessities. Near each of the homes there were small patches of land, some behind, in front, or alongside, where kitchen gardens were planted. They were well-tended, even though water often had to be hand-pumped. Family gardens produced most of the fruit, herbs and vegetables for the villagers' own tables for the whole year.

This was a busy, self-sufficient little town, its rhythm and pace steady and familiar. Five days were dedicated to work, one day was for personal business. Each Sunday began with church, followed by a parade of one's finery, weather permitting, and chatting with neighbors. The village's young men and women took the opportunity to look each other over.

Here, just as everywhere, a strong class structure dominated daily life. The village's business owners were rich, by their standards, and respected. They also filled most of the important official civic positions in the town. The mayor was the owner of the butcher shop. The town clerk, who was responsible for all of the village's records, was also proprietor of the most popular tavern. There was a cobbler to make and repair shoes and a seamstress who made clothes and altered and repaired them when necessary. For those folks who didn't make their own, there was a vintner who made the local wine, a baker, and a pasta and a cheese maker. There was a widow who made a living cooking for men who lived alone or for women who were too sick to cook for their families.

If a doctor was needed one lived in the next town, a dentist a bit farther away. The postman needed no other job, since the government paid him a steady, dependable salary for his services and he was accorded the respect the townspeople gave to all civil service employees. The village priest, too, needed no other means of support, since the townsfolk provided for all of the pastor's needed services or products. Indeed many of the villagers' own needs were often met through a barter system.

Chapter 5

One Family

Don Stephano Solicitto, the town clerk and owner of the tavern, was a short, big-bellied, self-satisfied man. In his official capacity he supervised the four people who worked in the records office at the town hall. He knew everyone's history. In his tavern, he ruled with a soft hand in a heavy leather gauntlet. He strutted like a peacock through this world that was his paradise. His wife was still a good-looking woman and in public, she pretended to obey his every order. She cooked well and had given him five sons. These five sons were obedient, somewhat complacent and still lived at home. Their greatest excitement came when they went hunting for game in the nearby hills. However, there was one bump in the road through, Don Solicitto's perfect world, his only daughter, pretty Josefina.

Josefina was the middle child. Because she was lively and lovely to look at, she was pampered by her father and brothers and by almost everyone around her. As she grew older however, behavior that was once cute became impudent -- and then arrogant, as she found that she could get away with more and more mischief because of her good looks.

Her mother kept a steady gaze and a firm hand on the girl, watching her grow prettier but stronger-willed as well. Josefina found it easy to charm or bulldoze the men in the family, and in the town too, but her mother could still keep her in line with a sharp glance.

As she approached the end of her teen years, Josefina's parents began talking about finding her a suitable husband. The village stock, they felt, offered little to their prize, their princess. Yet, since this was the only world they knew, they felt they had nowhere else to turn. The girl understood quite well what her parents were whispering, but Josefina, like her parents, hadn't found anyone to her liking among the village swains. She was quite satisfied with her status in the family and among her friends. Josefina felt no sense of urgency about her single status and was sure her prince would come – when she was ready.

Rumors of change, even war, had barely touched their community. Old customs, superstitions and beliefs were as new in Santa Teresa as in all the long years before. Life went on pretty much as it had for all the years before Mussolini became Il Duce. A few of the village's young men, those with some ambition, couldn't find anything they cared to do in Santa Teresa. They had gone to nearby Catania and other larger cities, some to enlist in the military or to seek work and had never returned. For Josefina, those who remained were, to her thinking, unrelated versions of her brothers. She found them dull, slow-witted and boring -- like her brothers but wearing different shirts.

Chapter 6

Someone New in Town

In Josefina's 19th summer, a visitor came to Santa Teresa. He was a man who had emigrated from Santa Teresa to America, not to seek his fortune but to run from the law after beating a neighbor nearly to death. He returned now and to some of the townspeople he was a sort of hero. His name, when he left Santa Teresa years before, was Giovanni Fiorelli. In America, his adopted country, Giovanni had found a use for his natural agility and strength. He'd become a professional boxer and had achieved the U.S. middleweight championship, fighting under the name Gerry Flowers. He had earned a measure of fame in the fight business after once beating the popular champion, Rocco Tarantino, as well as all the others in his weight class, to reach the top. Most of his one-time opponents had since become personal friends.

Now he had returned to the town of his birth to find a suitable wife. The house once owned by his grandfather had been sold after the old man died, so he rented a room in the boarding house run by the woman who cooked for bachelors.

"All the women in America are putanas," Gerry held forth at Don Solicitto's tavern, the evening after his arrival. His first language, the Italian spoken in this town was still easy on his tongue and was totally familiar to his rapt listeners. "They are either available for a price or will even spread their legs for a handsome man or a good-looking body," he told the admiring and titillated townsmen, as they sipped their wine and nodded their heads. "I need a pure Italian girl to be the mother of my children."

The Solicitto family, however, was neither impressed by nor interested in this man's needs. They feared he had an eye for their daughter. They did not want their child to leave the country, nor did they want American grandchildren. They had not forgotten why this wild boy had run away years before.

Josefina, who was just a baby when Gerry left the town, listened intently. She was drawn by his electric blue eyes, the long lashes, the wavy black hair, the powerful, vee-shaped, body. She thought the bent fighter's nose was a sign of virility and could understand why a woman might wish to "spread her legs" for him. Ah, yes, Josefina was in love.

When Gerry Flowers came into the tavern, she hurried to serve him his drink, something she had never done for anyone before. She brought a dish of olives, a basket of crusty bread and some olive oil with crushed garlic for dipping. Her father watched open-mouthed as his headstrong daughter played the role of a dutiful serving girl.

"Mama," he bellowed. His wife came out of the kitchen, wiping her hands on her apron. "We're in trouble," he said softly, nodding in his daughter's direction. His tired wife looked on as Josefina acted out a whole new role. Their strong-willed girl stood near the bar, her eyes downcast, lifting them only to steal glances at the stranger. She was one of the prettiest girls in town, slim-waisted, full-busted and utterly feminine.

Gerry had taken notice. He thought he saw a golden glow about the girl. He was impressed with her smooth, tawny skin, the glistening head of wavy, brown hair with sun glints of yellow, the wide brown eyes flecked with bits of gold, so warm and deep, the full mouth and round cheeks. But it was her downcast eyes and quiet demeanor -- a manner totally unfamiliar to her family and to the other men in the room -- that filled him with admiration.

After a few days, when he asked her to walk around the town with him, her mother made sure there were a few brothers trailing along at a polite distance. Josefina, star-struck and in love, listened raptly to his tales of life in New York. His stories opened a whole new universe for her on the dusty streets of Santa Teresa.

"I worked hard to get where I am as a boxer," he told her in his familiar dialect. "Now I can afford to keep a wife and a family in style. That's why I came back here, to find a good woman."

Throughout their walks and talks she held herself a bit aloof from him physically, always keeping a good distance between them, even though she yearned for his touch. She had heard his opinion of the easy women in America and was sharp enough to know that physical distance and a docile demeanor would provide the right route to his heart.

Chapter 7

Josefina Plots

After a few weeks, it was clear that the stranger was more than a little interested in this agreeable, very pretty and quite charming young woman. Josefina enjoyed having the townspeople see her with "the American." By then Josefina had made up her mind to have him as her husband. She didn't care a bit that it meant leaving her family and going to a new country. In fact, his stories about America excited her.

"Mama, when I move to America, I will send for all of you to live there with me," she told her mother. Her mother shrugged and reminded her daughter that she hadn't yet been asked.

"He will ask Papa for my hand very soon. You'll see," she said with her usual complete confidence and a toss of her head. That evening, when Josefina and Gerry went walking, she strolled a bit away from the town streets they usually walked, going to the edge of the sparse woods that bordered the village. She had convinced her brothers that she did not have to be watched so closely. They understood her hint, so they hung back farther than usual.

"I'm tired," she said, when her brothers were out of sight. "Let's sit." They sat on a large flat-topped rock alongside the dusty road. It was still warm from the afternoon sun. She gave him her full attention as she listened to him talk and then, as the sky darkened from a passing cloud, she gave a little shiver.

"Are you cold?" Gerry asked. "Just a chill," she replied. He put an arm around her shoulder and pulled her close. He could smell the lemony perfume of her shampoo, feel the satin smoothness of her sun-browned bare arm. It was the first time he had actually touched her and he became intoxicated with her intense femininity, immediately feeling its effect upon him in his groin.

"Cara, you are a beautiful, a wonderful woman. Will you be my wife? We could have a wonderful life together." He did not see the small smile of triumph as she answered him in a soft, modest voice.

"We'll have to see what my father says. He really doesn't want me to leave Santa Teresa, you know. He talks about how he wants to play with my children and all that."

"But Josi, how do you feel about me? Would you come with me to America even if he said no to my proposal?" He was growing more excited and animated as he spoke. "Josi, I love you, I need you and want you. Do you love me too?" he almost pleaded.

Her "yes" was barely a whisper. "I think I loved you right away when I first saw you," she whispered at his ear. Her lips touched his ear, her breath blew into his ear, her full breast rested on his chest as she turned to answer him. He found she aroused him as none of the women with whom he had made love did. He pulled her to him and kissed her lips, softly at first, then harder and then pressed his tongue between her lips.

Josefina was truly inexperienced and this kiss almost caused her to faint with the feelings it aroused in her. She pulled away with a gasp and leaned heavily against Gerry. He too seemed to be gasping for breath.

Chapter 8

Wedding Plans

"We must get back," she said. "My brothers will look for me soon if we don't return." As soon as she felt steady, she jumped up and began to walk back to the center of the village, with even more than the usual spring in her step. He followed, and when they reached the tavern, Josefina ran to her room but Gerry went immediately to speak with her father.

"Don Stephano, I asked your daughter to be my wife," he blurted. "May I have your blessing?"

Don Stephano, standing at the bar, polishing a glass, was surprised to see his daughter disappearing up the steps. He faced the almost distraught man who was making a proposal that was not entirely unexpected.

"Calm down. What's the hurry?" the Don asked, as he continued to rub the glass. "You only know her less than a month. How long did you plan to stay in Santa Teresa? Maybe you should go back to America and if you still want to marry her, come back next year. She's only 19 years old, you know. How old are you? What do you do besides fight, anyway? Is that a way to make a living? When you get old you can't fight anymore. Then what?" The questions went on until the suitor began to perspire.

"Hold it, old man. I love your daughter. I want to marry her. I am being honorable in this whole matter. What's your problem?" Gerry asked.

"She's my only daughter," the father answered. "If she goes away to America I know I'll never see her again. I love her too. And I want to be sure she is always properly taken care of. I don't know you at all. Maybe you'll beat her. She's not used to that, and you, a boxer, you could kill her. Why should I trust you? Sure any man would love her. She's a beauty, she has fire. Here, with my sons, I could make sure no one would hurt her. *That's* my problem, big shot. What do you say now?" the father said.

Chastened, Gerry said, "I meant no disrespect. You have a right to think about those things. Don Stephano, you knew my mother, she is a good woman. We live in a fine brick house that I bought for her. I make a good living and can give your daughter anything she wants. I would never hurt her and I want all the good things you want for her. If you know any people in New York, write to them, ask about me. I'm respectable and what I do is respectable. I'll wait here until they answer you."

Chapter 9

Celebration

A letter was written and sent and a response came two weeks later. In the meantime, Josefina mooned about, pecking at her food, crying for no reason until her father agreed to let her marry.

The wedding date was set for a month after the answering letter arrived. Gerry sent a ticket to his mother, who arrived in a state of excitement, about both the wedding and about seeing her home town and perhaps some friends again. She was invited to the homes of old friends as well as many of the people she had worked for. It was one of the happiest times of her life.

The Don, as town clerk and tavern owner, extended an open invitation to the whole town. The wedding was held on the cobblestone plaza in front of the tavern. Old Father Anselmo, who had christened both Gerry and Josefina, performed the ceremony. Tables were piled with fine food and wine, generously set out for all to partake. Three musicians, a fiddler, a concertina player and a trumpeter, played throughout the night. The dancing and drinking continued until the moon rose high in the night sky, its light competing with all the lanterns hanging from trees and from hooks on the buildings and set around on tables.

Halfway through the festivities, Gerry, flushed from dancing and a few glasses of wine, took Josefina by the hand and they slipped away to his boarding house room. It was much quieter there. Josefina was surprised to find that she was nervous. She thought that since this was what she had always wanted, it would be easy when the private time came. Not so.

Chapter 10

Learning Love

Gerry locked the door. He took his bride's hands and held her at arm's length. He looked at her in the shimmering satin bridal gown, her face reflecting the glow of the soft light from one small lamp. He pulled her close, tipped her face up and began kissing her, her eyes, her cheek, her jaw and finally her lips. He ran his tongue over her lips and then into her mouth. Josefina began to breathe harder. She could feel his fingers undoing the buttons on her gown. Her gown fell away. She stood in the lace bra and silk panties her mother had had made for this day. White silk stocking pressed into her thighs where fancy garters held them. She still had on the white satin slippers with high heels.

The sight of his bride exceeded all he had imagined. Gerry ran his hands down her back and circled her buttocks. He opened the bra and peeled it away. He backed away to look at the full firm breasts, white as milk since they'd never known the sun. He watched as the mauve-pink nipples stiffened. He took a round breast in each hand, kissed around the nipple and put one in his mouth and sucked. He removed the rest of her clothes. She stood with eyes closed, absorbing each new sensation with quivers of pleasure. He took off his shirt, took her hands and pressed them to his chest and then moved them down and led her hand to open his pants zipper while he undid the belt with the other. His trousers fell away. He slipped her hand into his underwear and wrapped her hand around his massive erection. His other hand reached into the down between her legs, a finger stroking her moist vagina. Josefina was mesmerized by all that was happening, overwhelmed by feelings entirely new, almost choking her.

All the girl knew about sex had come from sneaking looks at pictures in her brothers' rooms and from seeing farm animals copulate. And from reading some of the books she and her friends managed to get their hands on and from the talk they shared. But this was the first time she had been touched or had touched the sex of a man. She was filled with conflicting feelings. She was responding to the kisses but almost fearful of the throbbing penis in her hand – it seemed to have a life of its own.

"Please," she whispered, "more slowly. I don't know what to do."

Gerry was even more inflamed by this innocence, but knew he must control himself. He laid her down on the bed. Gently, slowly, he introduced her to the responsibilities of the marriage bed, and to its pleasures. He delighted in her moans and squeals, while she marveled at his cries, although she was not sure if they signaled pain or pleasure, both of which she had just experienced for the first time. After a while they fell asleep and slept deeply until the morning sun reached into the room, touching their eyelids, waking them like a silent alarm.

They dressed, she in the wrinkled bridal gown, and they went to join her family for breakfast. The landlady made sure the blood-smeared sheet was discretely passed around to approving family and friends.

Chapter 11

Carroll Gardens -- Newlyweds

Within a month Gerry and Josefina were settled into a house he bought in the Carroll Gardens section of Brooklyn. They'd found a handsome two-family brownstone on a quiet, tree-lined block in a mostly Italian neighborhood. Here Josefina found she could buy freshly baked Italian bread as good as that made in Santa Teresa, as well as freshly-made mozzarella cheese, pastas and sausages. An elderly Italian man came with an open truck piled high with fresh fruit and vegetables to sell, much of it from his own garden. Another truck, its open back lined with ice, brought fish to her door. All the familiar foods she knew, and many more that were new to her, were available and at hand.

A truly wonderful country, she thought, with satisfaction. She began to learn English words from her neighbors, who welcomed the pretty young bride. Before long she had girlfriends to sit on the stoop and talk with, to go to the stores with. Some of the women, whose husbands were making a good living loading ships on the nearby docks, took her to Macy's and Gimbels, wonderful places to shop for clothes. The nights were filled with lovemaking. Before the year was out she knew she was pregnant. Josefina knew she had made the right choice. She seldom thought of her family in Italy.

Gerry was ecstatic. He was going to be a father and his mother would become a grandmother. He took all the fights offered to him and sought out others he might not have taken, to earn as much money as he could. He had missed most of his formal education when he was taken out of school, but his "street smarts" served him well. The longer he fought the more he learned about finance and what was due him. He was now making "good" money.

Most nights after a fight he would go to unwind with a glass of wine. He would rehash the fight with his friends, other boxers, their women and their hangers-on. He often came home long after Josefina was asleep. He held the belief that a pregnant woman should not be in the fight and bar environment. He was away from home a great deal and did not comprehend that his wife was feeling left out of his life and somewhat neglected. He thought she would understand that when he was away it was for business – getting as much as he could while he could. She felt he should be at her side as her pregnancy progressed. The first time he failed to come home from an out-of-town bout the next morning, Josefina went to the police station in a panic, to report him as missing.

Since he was gone more than the required 24 hours, a detective took her information. He was a big, light-haired man who was sympathetic and listened carefully as the pretty young woman, speaking with a heavy accent, gave details through her tears. He reassured her that her husband would turn up fine.

"There are many things to delay a return from Ohio" he told her. We'll see what we can find out. When she arrived home, Jerry was waiting for her and embraced and comforted her. She called the station, asked for Detective Von Holsten and thanked him for his kindness.

Their son was born while Gerry had an important fight in Philadelphia. He went a day early to scout the arena and came back a day after the fight after checking with the doctors about a deep cut on his forehead. Gerry was elated by the large purse he had earned. He ran to the hospital to see his wife and son. He was delighted at the sight of the squalling infant, saw the crying as a sign of strength. When there he learned that the baby's birth certificate had already been filed and his son had been named Stephano, for his father-in-law. Gerry felt a small sting of resentment that his son had not been named for him or that Josefina felt she could not wait until he returned from Philadelphia before naming the child. When she saw his disappointment, Josefina felt a small tweak of satisfaction.

"If you were here for me to ask I guess he would be named for you," she was pleased to tell him. Each of them was looking at a different path.

Chapter 12

Changing Feelings

This was how Josefina expressed the nagging resentment because he had not returned immediately after the fight to be with her and to see the baby. She never asked him about his fights, or the occasional bandages he came home with. Other small resentments began building. She knew he never noticed how she had fixed the apartment, never cared what she cooked for his dinner. He took all these things for granted and never offered a compliment for what she had accomplished. Nor could he understand her loneliness when he spent days away, because he trusted her to know he was attending to business. She never questioned where he had been the extra days because she feared the answer, always suspecting other women. They both nursed their growing resentments in deep secret places inside themselves. Yet their daily life seemed to pick up almost as before, with just a bit less warmth, less intimacy.

One evening as he watched her nurse the baby, Gerry said, "Cara, you are a beautiful mother, a madonna." His heart filled with love and his body with lust. Later, in bed together, he reached for her, stroking a rounded, swollen breast, and began to lick and suck on a nipple. He was filled with the need for her body.

"Stop that," she hissed. "The baby needs the milk and my nipples are sore. You can't do that now." He felt slapped down, deflated. He turned away from her with a bitter taste in his mouth and another segment of their passion withered. Nevertheless their life resumed a regular pace and two years later their daughter, Maria, was born.

Chapter 13

Carroll Gardens – 26th Precinct

Officer O'Hara called for an ambulance while he waited for back-up from the precinct. He told the four spectators to stand out in the hall and not touch anything. Looking around at the scene O'Hara saw a nightclub photo of the dead man and woman propped up on the stove. On the table lay an empty bottle of iodine. He was beginning to get an idea of what had happened in that room. Moments later detectives from the precinct arrived.

"Did you touch anything?" they asked O'Hara.

"Yeah, I broke the window and shut off the gas," O'Hara said with a shrug. They nodded and began their investigation. After a while the detective who had been taking notes went into the hallway to speak to the people who were huddled there.

The tall, thin detective looked at the people in the hallway. The woman was good-looking, full-bodied, her head held high. He showed his gold shield before he spoke to the woman. He asked her name, what she was doing there and did she know the people in the room.

"My name is Josefina Fiorelli. That's my husband, Gerry Flowers," she spat out. "The other one is his *puta*, his whore."

Chapter 14

Giovanni, Santa Teresa

Giovanni Fiorelli was the only child of Concetta Fiorelli. He was an only child because her husband, his father, had died when he was just two years old. Giovanni Fiorelli, the father, had suffered a fatal heart attack at the age of 34. The young mother, after only three years of marriage was now a widow. Like all the widows in Santa Teresa, she put on her black dress, black stockings and black oxfords and wore that uniform for the rest of her life. She gave up the home her husband had hoped to buy for his new family and moved back into her father's house. Her mother had also recently died and she felt it would be the proper thing to do, to take care of her father.

Concetta was a talented seamstress and made enough money to run the house. When her father, Giovanni's grandfather, saw the money coming in, he no longer looked for work but spent his days at the tavern. Concetta doted on the baby, watching him grow from infant to toddler, lavishing all her unrequited need for affection and love on the child. He was a happy child, handsome and strong, and when time came to start school, he showed promise as a good student, a quick learner. He had friends to play with, a loving mother, and although his grandfather was a grumpy man, there was still the sense of a masculine presence. Things went well until Giovanni was ten. His mother suddenly began to ail and took less work. His grandfather railed against the child, saying he was soft and spoiled. He came home one day and said he had arranged for the grocer to give the boy a job.

Concetta fought against taking Giovanni out of school but the grandfather told them he could not support them and they would have to leave unless more money came into the house. He said school was a waste of time. So Giovanni's childhood came to an end and days of drudgery began for him. His only joy was to bring home his meager pay at the end of the week and present it to his mother, who now spent most of the day in bed. In the evening he sat with her and read from his old schoolbooks and from pieces of newspaper he salvaged from people's trash. Slowly, she regained her health but Giovanni kept on working at the grocery and never returned to school.

As he grew older, he gained physical strength from hefting cases of canned goods and racks of bottles. He reached his full height by the time he was 17. He was so handsome that girls in town turned to stare after him. Despite his dead-end job, Giovanni managed to keep a pleasant manner, especially with the women and girls who came into the store. When he could, he would meet one or another of the girls and carry on a harmless flirtation. When a father or brother learned that the girl was interested, they'd show up at the grocery and behave in a threatening manner and Giovanni no longer saw that girl.

He was still a virgin when one of the young women he bantered with was found to be pregnant. He had never been intimate with any girl but was accused of the deed. He and the girl both denied his paternity but she refused to name the father. One night soon after, her brothers waited for Giovanni. He was on his way home when they grabbed him. Two held him with all their might while a third battered him until he was bloodied and finally unconscious. When he came to, he dragged himself home. His mother was horrified. His face was battered and turning blue, his eyes nearly swollen shut, his mouth bleeding.

Chapter 15

Reversal

He'd been kicked and scratched and his clothes were torn. Concetta heated water and filled a tub. She washed and cleaned the blood and dirt that covered him from his hair to his feet. After he was abed, she knew that she had only cleansed the beating from his surface but had not soothed or washed away the fury and humiliation he was feeling inside.

When he returned to work the next week, he was no longer pleasant or communicative. He barely spoke to any customer and would not serve any of the young women who came into the store, mostly to see him. His anger festered. He kept a secret watch on the brothers and learned their routines. Weeks later, he waited for the brother who had beat him so savagely, knowing he would be returning alone from his girlfriend's house.

At a point in the road that was deserted at that time of the night, he grabbed and vented all his collected fury on the surprised man. He hit, slapped, punched and kicked ferociously until the fellow, who could only hold his hands up to protect himself from the barrage of blows, began to sag. He never had a chance to hit back and after a while he fell to the ground and did not move. Giovanni waited to see if he would get up, but the man was unconscious.

Giovanni ran home. He told his mother that he had killed the man who had beaten him. She panicked. She took a tablecloth and packed into it his small store of clothes. She loaded a flour sack with whatever food was on hand and gave him all the money she had saved. She told him to go to the harbor at Catania and get on a ship and save himself.

"Run away, maybe to America, my son. They won't look for you there. Write to me as soon as you can but use a different name." She kept giving advice until he walked out the door. She made the sign of the cross over him, kissed him and watched him run down the road until he was lost in the darkness. Then she allowed herself to weep for her unhappy child, wondering if she would ever see him again. He was the light of her life and now that light was disappearing, leaving her in the fierce gloom of a stormy night.

Chapter 16

Escape

Giovanni walked through the night in the direction he knew the big city lay. When the sun rose he burrowed into bushes at the side of the road and slept for several hours. At dark he began walking again, fearful of being discovered. He ate some of the food his mother had packed, used the forest for a toilet and washed wherever he found water as he continued his trek.

After three days he knew he was nearing Catania. Road traffic had increased, houses crowded closer together, growing larger and finer as he progressed. Soon he could see the spires of grand churches and finally the great round column that stood towering above the buildings in the town square. He had heard about this monument, with its elephant on top, and knew that it commemorated some historic victory. He had never seen such a city and because of the crowds, he walked without fear that he might be found out. He saw the ocean glittering in the distance and there were so many people going about their business that no one paid attention to the country bumpkin who now walked toward the waterfront.

When he reached the piers, he sat down on a keg and watched the action taking place around him. He saw ships, large and small, some even with sails. He saw men loading cartons and boxes onto tall ships, nets laden with heavy materials, being hoisted aboard. He saw men who were obviously seamen, with duffle bags slung over their shoulders, walking up gangplanks. He stared at his sorry-looking tablecloth and instinctively knew it identified him as a yokel. He opened the knots that tied the cloth and stuffed everything into one of the dark shirts his mother had packed. He tied the sleeves together and pulled at the bottom corners of the shirt and tied them together. He felt this bundle would be less noticeable.

After a while, he began talking to some of the people standing around. He learned the destinations of several of the ships, noted those bound for America. That evening he went to all that were heading for the land his mother had mentioned, to ask for work and passage. He asked at several that were westward bound but most had already hired all they needed. One that was ready to shove off always had a need for an extra hand and agreed to hire the healthy-looking youth, no questions asked.

Throughout the trip he worked continuously, tirelessly, pushing away all thought of what had happened, where he was going or what the future might hold for him. At night, in his bunk, he listened to the conversation of the men around him. They spoke of women, of work and of the wondrous city to which the ship would bring them.

Nothing he had heard prepared him for New York. He stepped off the ship, his hard-earned pay in his pocket, his few belongings now in a burlap sack.

The dockside was bustling with people. Longshoremen, with hooks tucked into their belts or over their shoulders, began the work of unloading. Giovanni slipped through them and headed for the streets. Buildings, higher than the cathedrals in Catania or any he had ever seen, shocked him. The streets were filled with automobiles, trolleys, buses and even some horse-drawn wagons. Pedestrians, seemingly bent on suicide, ran between the fast moving vehicles and miraculously came through alive. The din hurt his ears. The movement began to blur before his eyes. He stood open-mouthed, bewildered.

He listened, then asked directions from speakers of Italian and found the Fulton fish market. The men on board ship had said there was work there and he wandered around the waterfront until he saw the stalls and doorways laden with boxes of fish. He looked about for someone to speak with but couldn't decide who might help. He heard Italian being spoken, heard a familiar dialect, then found the speaker and asked about a job. The man went with him to a fellow who stood at a dais, writing in a ledger. After some discussion, the man said it would cost $20 for him to work. This was standard procedure but it would exhaust almost all of the money he had earned for all the weeks on the ship. The man quickly pocketed the cash.

He started work right then and there and worked steadily for the next eight or nine hours. He had not eaten or rested since leaving the ship. When the day was done he waited in line to be paid, then walked away, dazed with exhaustion, with no destination. He came upon a street vendor, bought a frankfurter, which he thought was a sausage, and wolfed it down. He walked further until he was in a quiet, darkened neighborhood, found a doorway and fell asleep. This was his entry into America.

Chapter 17

The New Country

The next day a co-worker steered him to a tenement where he could rent a room cheaply. He shared the space with a man named Hans, and was grateful there were two beds in the room. The bathroom was out in the hallway and was shared with several other men on the floor. Everyone was expected to clean his own space. His day-to day existence was smelly drudgery but he was putting money aside from his paltry salary, with the goal of sending for his mother. If he could accomplish that he would worry about what came next. He put the money in a sock and hid it in the pocket of one of his old shirts.

His roommate, Hans, who had come from Germany, worked in a bakery and he was allowed to take home leftover day-old bread, rolls and buns. With these he made sandwich suppers. Never did he offer any to Giovanni, who would have made the plain bread his meal. Giovanni called Hans a cheapskate – one of the new words he was learning every day. To save money he walked through nice neighborhoods and looked in the rubbish bins behind stores to find food that had been discarded but was still edible. He found that people threw away perfectly good clothes and other items that he took home, washed and used.

As his sock bank became heavier he made trips to the steamship office to check on ticket prices. Sometimes, at night, he would take out the money to see if there was enough. When there finally was, he wrote to his mother and told her the next letter would bring her a ticket to America and to his side.

That night, after work, he went to get the money. He couldn't find the sock in the shirt pocket where he had left it and began to pull all of his belongings apart, on the chance he had moved it and somehow forgotten where he put it. When he was exhausted, he sat down on the bed, his head in his hands. He looked around the room and finally noticed that Hans' belongings were nowhere to be seen. He looked under Hans' bed and saw his suitcase was gone. In his frenzy and confusion he had never seen that Hans had cleared out. It was then he realized he'd been robbed.

Before dawn he went to the bakery where Hans worked. Hans was still there but refused to come out to speak with him. Giovanni ran to the back room and grabbed Hans by the collar.

"You stole my money, you thief," he screamed. Anger made Giovanni's eyes bug out and his face flushed almost purple. He looked like a wild man. "Give me back my money or I'll kill you." Suddenly he was surrounded by three other bakers, brandishing pans and rolling pins.

Hans sneered at him, brave because of the support from his fellow bakers. "You greenhorn, I didn't take nothing from you. You're a dummy and you don't know how to live in a free country. You even eat garbage."

Giovanni lost control. He picked up a rolling pin from the counter in front of him and began swinging it at all the men around him. He had the advantage of fury and surprise and managed to knock some of the weapons from their hands. They backed off and he grabbed Hans and began beating him. Months of heavy work had toughened him and built on his natural strength. When added to his anger, it became impossible for his opponent to get a hand on him. When Giovanni had beaten Hans to the ground and bloodied his face, the others pulled him off. "That's enough," they said.

Giovanni's knuckles were raw and bleeding. The other man, almost unconscious, did not move. He went through Hans' pockets and pulled out the sock, with the money intact. The others backed off, shamefaced at the thievery of their colleague.

Chapter 18

New Ideas

The owner of the bake shop looked at the carnage. "Why don't you fight someone your own size and strength, you bully. Get out of here before I call the cops."

Giovanni cared nothing about the police or the baker's threats now that he had his money back. He went to the steamship office, disheveled and smeared with blood, and bought the ticket. It was not until that night, after he had mailed the ticket to his mother, that he thought about what the bakery owner had said about fighting.

Suddenly, just like in the funny papers he'd found in some of the trash cans whose pictures he tried to follow, a light bulb seemed to click on in his head. He had heard some of the men he worked with talk about "the fights." He knew they paid good money to watch men beat each other up and made wagers on who would win -- and he had heard that the fighters were paid, whether they won or lost.

When he returned to his room that night another man had rented the share vacated by Hans. This man was about 30 years old, an Italian from Palermo. Giovanni spoke with him about Italy, about the trip to America and about the fights.

"You want to fight?" the man asked. "You'll get knocked on your ass and mess up your pretty face. It's not for pretty boys like you. Tough guys like me, maybe, but kids like you, forget it." Giovanni was a naïve 17-year old but thought he knew better.

Chapter 19

A New Career

He could not be talked out of trying and began to ask around about where to go to become a boxer. A few nights later, before going home he wandered into a gym along the waterfront. There he spoke to some of the young men. They wore thick mittens and punched heavy bags and small, ball-shaped bladders that jumped back at them. They were not talkers and didn't tell him much, but a conniving trainer-manager, a short, balding, pigeon-shaped man named Chippy Mangione watched as he walked around, seeking information. He saw a hungry youth where others saw a pretty boy. He saw possibilities in the sturdy body and graceful moves. Mangione, on his skinny pigeon legs, strutted over to Giovanni.

"Let's see what you got, kid," Mangione said. He outfitted Giovanni with shorts, shoes and gloves and sent him into the ring to spar. His sparring partner, a gym hack and long-time loser, thought he would have some fun pushing the handsome boy around, giving back some of what he had to take most days. He couldn't know about the anger percolating through the young man for the hundreds of slights, both real and imagined, that he'd suffered. Therefore, he was totally unprepared for the barrage of fists that fell on his body and face in just minutes, or the quickness of the young legs that danced around his slow-moving form. Mangione, however, saw potential -- and heard the *ka-ching* of money.

That's how and when Giovanni Fiorelli became Gerry Flowers. Giovanni worked at the fish market during the day and trained, passionately, all evening. After four months of training in the fine art of professional boxing under the tutelage of Chippy Mangione, he had his first fight. His opponent was a beat-up boxer on the way out of the game, just as the newly-named Gerry was stepping in. Gerry beat him easily and went on to win every fight he was in until the end of the year and beyond. By the time he was 21 he was ready for some serious contenders. His first loss came at the hands of a hard-fisted, old-time professional. This loss diminished some of the cockiness he was developing and made him train harder, longer and better. Soon he was getting matches that would lead to the top boxers in his weight class. He was earning enough now to give up his job at the fish market.

Chapter 20

A New Life

Gerry Flowers, while learning a new trade was learning a new life style too. Even though his manager was pocketing far more of the winnings than Gerry did, he had more money than he ever imagined he would own. He bought and furnished a small house for his mother in Bensonhurst, a nice, heavily Italian neighborhood in Brooklyn. There was even a rent-paying tenant to cover expenses. Both he and his mother were both still village rubes enough to feel amazed at being landlords of a fine brick building in this fantastic new land.

His new friends were men who lived higher and faster than anything he had known before. Most were other fighters, some comers like himself, some old-timers and some, just hangers-on who were on hand for a drink and good fight talk. There were also a few aspiring show people who stopped to sit at his table when he hit the nightclubs. Women flocked to him and were easy to bed. People even asked for his autograph. When he stopped to think he couldn't believe what had happened to his life.

Gerry lived a cleaner life than most of his associates because he still tried to please his mother. He never brought women home, never came home drunk. Friends were invited to his house and he was proud to introduce them to his mother. His new buddy, Rocco Tartaglia, would come to eat his mother's good cooking and sometimes sleep on their sofa when Rocco's girlfriend Mona was angry with him and wouldn't let him into her bed. Rocco had a wife and son but spent most of his time with his lover, Mona. Many of the men in his circle had girlfriends, even the married ones.

At the age of 24 Gerry won the championship in the light-heavyweight division and still held it two years later. His nose had been broken several times but his face was still good-looking. He was making a good living and was a sharp dresser in tailor-made suits that fit his body as though the fabric had been melted and poured on. He always wore a silk handkerchief in his breast pocket that matched his tie. Through it all he remained, what everyone called him, "a really nice guy." That was when his mother began her marriage crusade.

Chapter 21

The Search

"I want to live to see grandchildren," Concetta said. "You should be looking for a wife," was the sermon his Mama would preach and serve with his Sunday breakfast. His mother remembered the joys of her short marriage and wanted that for her beloved son. He thought of the women with whom he had been meeting and sleeping. In the crowd he ran with there was not one he would bring home to meet his mother.

"Mama," he said, "there's no one decent out there. The women are wild. You would not want to be their mother-in-law. You'd be ashamed."

"Well, you could go back to Italy to find a virgin girl from a good family," she suggested. He wondered if he would get arrested if he returned. He'd known for a long time that the man he had beaten had not died but had recovered, married and moved to another town .

"Nobody even remembers what you did," his mother assured him, "and now you are rich and important. You could get a good girl." He did finally feel good about himself and had always trusted his mother's judgement. He was getting tired of the so-called high life and wanted to settle down. If he went back to the old country and found a pure and honest woman, a woman like his mother, he would get married. That's what took him back to Santa Teresa that summer, the only town he really knew in Italy, to Josefina, and to his fate.

Chapter 22

Carroll Gardens – Ten Years Later

"Yeah, I broke the window and shut off the gas," Officer O'Hara said with a shrug. The detectives nodded and began their investigation. After a while the tall, thin one who had been taking notes went into the hallway to speak to the people who were huddled there.

"I'm Detective Harley," the lanky man said quietly. "Who are these gentlemen?" he queried and pointed to the three men standing in the hall with Josefina.

"Dey are my brodders," she replied, her Italian accent thickening. "Dey lives inna da donnastairs apartment."

"And do you live here in this apartment?" the detective asked the woman, pointing into the kitchen. She nodded yes. "Where were you all evening?" he asked.

"I was by my friend, then I came home and went in to see my brothers," she answered. "I didn't know they was here," she jerked a thumb in the direction of the bodies.

The ambulance pulled up and white-coated attendants ran up the stairs, carrying a stretcher.

"We think she might still be alive," O'Hara said. Everyone stopped talking. The ambulance attendant bent over the woman, adjusted a stethoscope and listened for a heartbeat. He heard nothing. "No, she's gone," the attendant said.

"Good," said Josefina with a sneer. She turned away from the detective and gestured to her brothers to go downstairs. They trooped down the steps, silently, in single file.

Harley, surprised by her curt remark and by the unexcused departure, called after her, "We'll be down to talk to you in a few minutes."

Chapter 23

Gigi

Gertrude Whiteman was the fifth daughter in a family of six girls. Her father, Reuven, an orthodox Jew, was unhappy because there would never be a son to say kaddish, the Hebrew prayer for the dead, for him when he died. But after six girls his wife had refused to consider further pregnancies and he had given up hoping for a boy.

It wasn't easy for Reuven, living with seven women. His wife, Malka, and each of the six daughters had a distinct and different personality. Just the daily living in this house of women presented problems for him. For instance, going into the bathroom was like entering a nylon jungle. Seven pairs of nylon or silk stockings hung from the shower bar every evening. If his head got too close, a stocking would catch onto and stick in his hair and be pulled from the bar. And he had learned, after years of yelling, "Stop that," at the bickering girls, to ignore the almost constant yammering which he called "their nonsense."

The girls hated their given names, Hannah, Velma, Martha, Mildred, Gertrude and Louisa. In their teens each had adopted a nickname by which they would be known for the rest of their lives. Gertrude, next to last, hated when anyone called her Gertie or Trudy. She became Gigi after she read the story by Colette and the nickname really took hold after the movie with Leslie Caron.

Gigi was the tallest in a family of short people. She was five feet six inches tall and towered over her Papa and Mama, who both only skimmed five feet. From age nine until she reached 14 she, more than the other girls, went through an awkward stage. None of the parts of her face seemed to fit right. Her legs and arms seemed too long for her body. Before her fifteenth birthday, her skin was sallow, she was too skinny, and her dark hair hung lankly. However, the huge, deep, dark eyes that filled her face held a promise of the beauty to come.

At 15, Gigi, along with her new name, metamorphosed like a butterfly bursting out of a cocoon. Her body developed luscious curves, her waist whittled down to 18 inches, and she developed shapely, race-horse-muscled legs. All the awkwardness had disappeared from her face as well. A wide, clear forehead and high cheekbones tapered into a perfect heart-shape. Her lips and her hair became thick and full, her nose, always small, thin and tilted slightly, fit her newly shaped face perfectly. The big, almost jet-black eyes were still the most striking feature and fulfilled their earlier promise. With her dark hair parted in the middle she was a ringer for an old-time actress, Hedy Lamarr, and the prettiest of the six girls, though all were attractive. Gigi had an adventurous sense of style, too, lots of flair in the way she wore clothes.

Of them all, Gigi was the toughest and most rebellious of the Whiteman girls. She fought with her mouth and her hands to hold on to what she felt belonged to her. This attitude was alien in a household where almost everything was a hand-me-down and what belonged to one belonged to all -- and where no one had ever raised a hand in anger.

Chapter 24

The Whiteman Family

Mama Malka Whiteman, still a beautiful woman, had fought with poverty all her life, sometimes losing, occasionally winning some small battles. Her husband, Reuven, was the only sibling in a family of ten children to come to America from Poland. He had never worked in the old country but had spent his youth studying Torah, the holy scrolls and reading religious tracts. When he arrived in New York, a landesman, (a fellow townsman from Poland) helped him find a job in a factory, sewing coats. The townsman also introduced him to Malka, the sister of a woman he was dating. Reuven Whiteman fell instantly and deeply in love with Malka. Both still virgins, there was no romancing and their first kiss was at their wedding. He married her after a year of dating and their family began its increase within the next year.

Malka was a careful manager and ran a satisfactory household. Over time, her own experience with marriage gave birth to a philosophy as well as to a family. She used this philosophy to relentlessly tutor her six daughters. It was a drill they would hear from earliest childhood, a refrain that became as familiar as breathing.

"A woman's lot in life is to marry and have children," Mama Whiteman told them. "Everything else is extra, nothing else is important. But remember, it's as easy to love a rich man as a poor one," continued the mantra. "So look to marry a man with a lot of money. If you can't grab a rich one, then he must at least have a good steady job. A husband should have both parents, because otherwise he has to take care of his mother and that takes away from you and your family. It's nice for you to have an education," she cautioned, "but it shouldn't get in the way of getting married." There was more.

"If you can't get the man you want, then accept a man you can get. Looks are not important because they change pretty fast. *Love,*" she grimaced, meaning passion, "flies out the door in six months anyway, so sometimes it's better to marry a nice person that you can learn to like. It's a strange thing," she mused, "the minute you're not a virgin anymore you see things different. Like when a man breaks your hymen, it clears your eyes. And your brain."

Chapter 25

Customs

The sisters grew up hearing this wisdom, early and often. As each reached the marriageable age of 17, the husband hunt began. The girls were all pretty, but mostly naïve and unworldly. Nevertheless, dates abounded and the oldest was wed by the time she was 19. Then the family sold their house in Queens and moved into a four-bedroom apartment near Southern Boulevard in the Bronx. The parents used one bedroom. Four of the sisters agreed to share the two other large rooms and Gigi stormed until she got the last bedroom, a small cell of a room, for herself.

The first of the six daughters to marry had the most lavish wedding. It was held at the Concourse Plaza Hotel, *the place* for weddings in the Bronx. No expense was spared and it was a gala affair. Now there were five at home. The next daughter was married at home, the food catered in, the furniture pushed against the wall so the guests could dance to the music of the radio. The third daughter eloped and was married in Elkton, Maryland. However, Malka insisted on a religious ceremony and both ceremony and dinner were held in a neighborhood restaurant. The fourth daughter's nuptials were held in the same restaurant as the third sister's. Gigi's wedding was the fifth and held – again in that familiar restaurant. By the time the last daughter was married it was in the basement of a local synagogue, the cooking done by a culinarily-talented cousin and set up as a buffet. There was a three-piece band for that one, a trio of neighbors' sons who had formed a put-together band, so there was dancing. A cousin took a few pictures of the joyous event.

They danced the Mazinka, a dance signifying the last child's wedding. Malka breathed a deep sigh of relief.

Gigi, strong-willed and determined, had quit high school the day she turned 16, the legal age for departure from school and got a job at the local Woolworth's. When she got her first paycheck she put a lock on the door of her room. Papa Whiteman was shocked and made her remove it, so she put it on her closet door and there it stayed. After years of hand-me-downs and a busy household, she was obstinate about her personal space and possessive of her purchases.

With her earnings she bought the clothes she wanted and put them under lock and key so that no one could get near them. She didn't let anyone wash or iron her things although she would help with everyone elses'. She was meticulous about her person and her belongings, her room was spotless and tidy. She could always tell if anyone had gone into it and ranted about needing her privacy.

Gigi's job at the Woolworth was behind the candy counter. When a family member or friend came in for candy she always gave them more than she charged them for, her way of rebelling against the low wage. She spent her days at work and her evenings going dancing or hanging out at an ice cream parlor-luncheonette on Southern Boulevard, a wide avenue filled with stores, ballrooms, restaurants and other commercial properties. The luncheonette was a huge store that served breakfast, lunch and dinner, but after the dinner hour it was a meeting place where masses of youngsters congregated. The juke box blared all evening and the kids could sit for hours with a cherry coke or an egg cream soda. That's where the "hip" crowd hung out.

Chapter 26

Meeting "the One"

Gigi had her eye on a boy who had just graduated from high school and was planning to go into "show biz." He was a crooner who sounded a lot like a popular singer of the time, Dick Haymes. He wasn't having much luck finding work since Dick Haymes was already famous and no one was looking for another sound-alike or a look-alike.

The boy's name was Seymour Goldberg but he called himself Gary Stark. Gigi thought he was gorgeous and let him know how she felt. Gary agreed with her assessment of his charms and they became an item. Gary was one of six brothers, just as she was one of six sisters, so she was sure fate meant for them to be together. He wallowed in her open adoration. She never noticed that it was neither mutual nor returned. Gary had one love, himself, so he welcomed the fan.

In time Gary got a few gigs, singing at weddings, christenings and bar mitzvahs, and a few times with a band at a small club, the Country Cabin, in New Jersey. She went along on his jobs to share the glory. Every penny he made went back into and onto himself. He bought the latest style suits, fine shirts and ties, good shoes. Gigi paid her own way wherever they went.

"In this business you really have to look sharp," Gary told Gigi. She agreed. They dated this way for a year and by then she wanted more than a pat on the head and a goodnight kiss.

"I think we should get married," Gigi announced one evening on their way back from a wedding job. He was 21 and Gigi was almost 17. Gary was shocked by the pronouncement. He stammered, "But, but,

but – I don't think we can. I don't have a steady job, we don't have any money. How would we live? Where would we live? "

Gigi had already given these questions much thought. She told him, "My parents will make a wedding." It was customary for people they knew to give cash gifts. A friend had told her about a studio apartment they could rent cheaply. She would keep on working while he went on auditions and the money he made from his gigs would keep them ahead when things got tight. They would be on their own and be able to do what they wanted. The idea sounded good to Gary and he loved the fact that she had taken charge of all the details. Now they had to convince their parents. Papa and Mama Whiteman, in tandem, immediately said a resounding "No!" They could see the young man for what he was, a selfish, self-aggrandizing loafer who would never get a "real" job. They could also foresee their most beautiful, capable, not quite 17-year-old daughter turning into a drudge, working to support a lazy but fancy bum.

"But I love him," Gigi moaned and wept. "I can't live without him," she wailed and keened. "I'll kill myself if we can't get married," she threatened. And although they didn't believe she would kill herself, they feared her obstinate nature and worried that she would somehow harm herself. She might even stop eating, heaven forbid! Gary's folks were so busy with their other five sons and their families, they hardly heard or cared when he said he wanted to get married. Knowing their son, they just hoped the girl was rich enough to take care of his needs.

Chapter 27

Gigi's Wedding

Gigi got her wedding, rented the studio apartment. She took furnishings and household appliances from anyone who wanted to get rid of a piece of furniture, an old toaster or some linens. Gigi painted the old furniture, made curtains from bits of fabric she found in her mother's house and turned the dark little one-room studio room into a pretty home. Her meager salary just paid for the room and the utilities. The wedding gifts helped when cash was in short supply – as when Gary needed another suit or new shoes. She brought food home from her mother's house or they ate at Gary's mom's home.

In a short eleven months after their wedding she gave birth to a baby boy they named Larry. With more cash gifts they bought a second-hand crib and a few other baby needs. However, Gigi with a new baby to take care of, could not go back to work. No one offered help and Mrs. Whiteman still had several daughters at home to take care of, so there was no one available to care for little Larry. The money from Gary's gigs wasn't enough to pay for anything but his own needs. The wedding money was quickly used up. They had to give up their little studio apartment.

Gigi, with baby Larry, returned to her mother's house, and now that two of her sisters had married and moved out, was able to take one of the larger rooms. Gary went back to his mother's house, although he could have shared Gigi's three-quarter bed and stayed with his new family. But the baby's crying disturbed his sleep and thus interfered with his "career." He also resented the time Gigi spent attending to the child rather than to him.

Gary had nothing to contribute, financially or emotionally to the relationship. Gigi, lonely and disillusioned, was coming to believe that the matrimonial advice she'd heard from her mother while growing up was correct. Gary no longer looked as good to her as he once did and she could now recognize his selfishness through the "clear eyes" her mother had predicted would come with the loss of virginity.

Gary did visit, but not often. He was too busy making the rounds of auditions and doing some writing and arranging. One day he came in to see Gigi, jubilant. He had written a song about "My Little Guy," their son Larry, that he was able to sell to a record company. It would be on the flip side of a "single," a record made by a popular singer. He would make some money from every record sold. "We're on our way," he said.

Chapter 28

More Life Changes

What Gary meant was that he was on his way. Whatever monies were realized from the record sales, which were good, none ever reached Gigi. Gary refurbished his wardrobe and began buying recording equipment which he set up at his mother's home. He began getting jobs arranging music for other singers and for some bands. He had found his niche -- music arranging -- was good at it and got so busy he had no time for a wife or a child. Gigi and the baby rarely saw him after that.

Since another of the Whiteman girls had gotten married after Gigi moved back home, Mrs. Whiteman was more willing and able to help with the care of little Larry. He was an adorable child who'd thrived on his mommy's care and attention. So Gigi thought about going back to work and went job hunting. She was hired at the "5 & 10" where she had originally worked when she quit school. The pay wasn't much but the store was close to home so she could run back to feed Larry his lunch and be just steps away if needed. Having some money in her pocket gave her a feeling of independence.

One afternoon a beautiful woman came over to her candy counter.

"Gigi, what are you doing here?" the woman asked. Gigi tried to place her but couldn't identify her.

"Do I know you?" Gigi asked.

"Oh, for goodness sake, Gigi, it's me, Bunny." Gigi's mouth dropped open.

"Bunny, you look gorgeous. You're so glamorous. What did you do?" she asked. Bunny Taylor was one of the girls who had hung out with her group at the luncheonette. She was a year or two older than Gigi. Her hair, now a tawny gold, was rolled into a glistening pompadour on top, the rest cascading to her shoulders to end in a page boy. She was fully made up and even seemed to be wearing false eyelashes. She looked like a star in a movie magazine.

"It's makeup, honey. A beauty parlor can do wonders with a little hair bleach and styling – and voila – the new me. But back to you. What happened with you and that Gary creep? Are you still together? And why are you back working here, for goodness sake?"

Suddenly, the floor manager stood next to Bunny. "Is anything wrong Madame?" he wanted to know.

Gigi giggled at Bunny being called Madame and the manager gave her a nasty glare. Bunny looked down her nose and said, "My good man, this woman is much too talented to work here. I'm sure you don't pay her enough and you work her too hard."

Gigi was shocked and shook her head from side to side. "No, no Mr. Williams, this is an old friend and she's just kidding. Everything's fine, really."

"Well," said Mr. Williams, "she just may be right. Why don't you pack your things and leave."

Gigi looked bereft, but Bunny said, "C'mon, let's get out of here. I want to talk to you. Slowly, with trepidation, Gigi packed her meager belongings, and told the manager she wanted the pay she was due for the time she had put in. She went to the office, picked up the paltry check and left with Bunny.

Chapter 29

A New Direction

They went to the same old luncheonette they used to hang out in and Bunny ordered sundaes for both of them.

Dizzy with the speed of all that had just happened, "I can't afford a sundae," Gigi whined.

"I can," said Bunny "and I want to talk to you about working. You know what I do? I'm a dancer, a showgirl in a night club. I work in clubs all over the city. And I love it. My boss is looking for a new girl for the chorus line. Why don't you try out for it?"

"I can't do that kind of dancing," Gigi said. She had always been a good dancer, but that was at Roseland, the Savoy Ballroom, Hunts Point Palace or one of the other dance palaces around the city.

"Listen, I have to go to rehearsal at 2:00 o'clock," Bunny told Gigi. "Come along and try out. What have you got to lose. You're not working now anyway," she said with a laugh. Gigi didn't think it was funny but agreed that she had nothing to lose by trying. She did need a job.

"I have to tell my Mom I'm going, and for her to feed my baby if I don't get back on time."

Bunny looked shocked. "You have a baby? When did that happen?"

Proudly, Gigi told her about 9-month-old Larry, then about having to go back to live in her mother's home.

"Let's go," said Bunny. "You need some fixing up before we go anyway." They returned to the Whiteman apartment. Bunny held the

54

baby on one arm while she pushed through the sparse but neatly hung clothes in Gigi's closet.

"Not much here for where we're going." Handing the baby to Gigi, Bunny pulled out a peasant-style embroidered blouse and a slim-skirted red velvet suit. Gigi had not worn these clothes since before her pregnancy. There'd been no place to go for a long time for which she needed to dress up. But she was even thinner than before she'd married and everything fit.

Chapter 30

Transformation

Bunny went to work on Gigi. The dancer's big black tote bag contained, among other things, all her make-up. First a coating of pancake make-up brightened Gigi's pale skin. Then she added a brush of rouge just under the high cheekbones and a dusting of powder. Bunny brushed the eyebrows into a fine line, pencilled a black line around the eyelids, added a soft grey eye shadow. She stopped at that point, took out something from the big bag, wrapped in aluminum foil . It was a metal spoon and a stick of what looked to Gigi like a black wax candle. Bunny broke off a chunk of the wax and put it into the bowl of the spoon, then lit a wooden match, held it under the spoon until the wax melted to a liquid. She took another brush and dipped it into the wax, blew on it and, holding Gigi's eyelid, applied the melted wax to her lashes, making them thick, long and prominent. She pulled out several tubes of lipstick then used a thin brush to apply a bright red lipstick that would pick up the red in the velvet suit. That finished the make-up. Bunny picked up the hair brush that sat on the dresser. "Take the rubber band off your pony tail, bend over and brush all the hair forward." Gigi bent at the waist and brushed her long brown hair down. "Okay, now stand and flip it back," ordered Bunny. The hair fell around her shoulders, thick and full, framing the newly-painted face.

"Take a look," Bunny said, leading Gigi to the mirror. All the while Bunny had been redecorating Gigi, Mrs. Whiteman, with Larry in her arms, had been standing in the doorway, watching as though at the theater. The baby thought it was funny until his Mommy turned into someone he didn't recognize and began to cry. The change was astounding. Both Mrs. Whiteman and Gigi were stunned by the new look, the glamour, as she stood before the mirror.

"Okay, do you have a pair of black heels?" Bunny wanted to know. It's time to go. Gigi slipped on a pair of stiletto pumps and realized they were a bit tight. She'd been wearing "comfortable" shoes for more than a year.

Chapter 31

To the Dance

"I hope I can walk in these," Gigi said. She and Bunny left the apartment and when they reached the street Bunny flagged a taxi. This was the first taxi Gigi had ever ridden in and she was growing ever more impressed by Bunny, by her good looks, her poise and the way she seemed to know her way around. Obviously, she had money – otherwise who could afford to take a cab?

They got to Manhattan in what seemed like minutes, while Gigi spoke about her marriage, separation, childbirth and her life from the last time she'd seen Bunny. Gigi was now 19 years old. In turn, Bunny, two years older, brought Gigi up to date on her life and what was happening with all the other kids who had hung out at the luncheonette. Gigi hadn't had that much fun in the last few years.

The practice studio was in an office building on 47th Street, off Broadway. Several "girls" were already there, some in shorts and polo shirts, others in loose slacks and sweaters. Bunny changed into a pair of shorts and a man-tailored shirt that she tied at the waist, pulled her hair back into a pony tail and put on dance shoes. She introduced Gigi to some of the other women. Two men came into the room. One, a gray-haired, well-built fellow of about 50, went to the front of the room, the other, younger, with a head of messy brown hair, sat down at the piano.

"Okay, ladies, let's go. Into line and into position," the older man commanded. Gigi sat down on a folding chair against the wall, watching, wide-eyed and intent. The music began and the gray-haired man led the group in a routine with which they all seemed familiar. The rehearsal went on for two hours, with many of the movements repeated until the choreographer was satisfied.

Chapter 32

Approved

When it was over, the women let out a collective whoosh of breath and some doubled over, letting their arms hang to the floor. Others swung their heads from left to right, loosening up and wiping perspiration with towels pulled from their huge tote bags. Bunny signaled Gigi and together they went over to the instructor.

"Lou, this is my friend Gigi. She's always been a great dancer and she's looking for a job. Do you think you might give her an audition to see if she can fill in for Joan?" asked Bunny.

Lou didn't answer. He backed away and looked Gigi up and down and from side to side. "Turn around," he said. Gigi turned.

"Have you had any experience in the line," he asked. She shook her head, no. "Speak up. You never danced professionally?" Have you studied dance?" Lou asked. She answered no in a small voice, her hopes dropping. Lou looked over at Bunny and lifted a questioning eyebrow.

"Give her a chance, Lou. She can do it and she needs the job. She's got a kid to raise," said Bunny.

Lou turned to Gigi. "You watched what the girls did, right? You heard my instructions. Do you have other clothes you can put on? I'll see how you follow my instructions."

Bunny said, "I'll give her some of my stuff, give us a minute." A few moments later, they came out from behind a screen, Gigi in a tee shirt and shorts from Bunny's voluminous tote bag and wearing Bunny's dancing shoes.

Josefina's Honor

"Okay, kid, let's see what you can do," Lou barked, and began calling the routine. Bunny, barefoot, worked alongside her, even though Lou frowned at her. Gigi had watched closely when the others had rehearsed. She had a natural rhythm and a good memory for steps. She followed the routine with hardly a misstep.

"Ya got a job, kid. It's twenty bucks a night when we have a gig. We pay for the costumes. Ya gotta be on time and that means in the dressing room at 7:30 tonight. I see you know how to do the make-up," all this said at machine gun speed from Lou. Bunny hugged Gigi, then Lou and said, "Thanks, Lou. See you tonight."

Chapter 33

The New Dancer

Gigi was stunned. "I'm hired? Just like that. Now I'm a dancer? Wow. All the way back to the Bronx the two women talked about the new beginning and its possibilities . When she got home she told her mother about her new job. She was so excited, she couldn't understand why her mother frowned at the news.

"Mama, I'll be working when it's practically little Larry's bedtime. It'll be so much easier for you. And twenty dollars a night, my goodness, that's almost double what I was making at the 5 & 10 in a week. Why aren't you happy?"

"Listen, Gertrude, since when are you a dancer?" Her mother admonished, "you're gonna be meeting low class people in those clubs. Who knows what they expect from you? Malka Whiteman had either plain common sense or perhaps the power of prophecy.

But Gigi wouldn't be dissuaded nor discouraged. She danced that night and a few nights the next week. In between taking care of her chores at home she learned the routines, wearing her old shorts and tops. She was fitted for new costumes. She became a part of the line on the stage of a succession of small clubs in Manhattan, Queens and Brooklyn, occasionally even the Bronx. The work went well and by 1:00 a.m. most nights, she was in a cab with Bunny heading home. She was up early to give Larry his breakfast and played with him until he was ready for his nap. She found she was tired too, and napped along with him.

Mrs. Whiteman grumbled about the late homecoming but saw

her daughter blossoming. Gigi was more self-assured and seemed to be enjoying her job immensely, something Mrs. Whiteman found difficult to understand. Who liked work?

Chapter 34

Women at Work

Gigi couldn't wait to go to work at night. She enjoyed the ambience, the excitement of the clubs, preened at the attention, and most of all was stunned at the money she was making for dancing – an activity she had always loved. In just weeks she was a professional part of the line-up, learning all the new routines as fast as the best of them. Putting on the stage make-up was fun, like painting a picture, and she enjoyed the finished product. Her posture became more confident, she moved like a dancer. She and Bunny made friends with some of the other women and like most of them, she began spending an hour or so after the show sitting with customers at the clubs. In time she dated some of those customers and didn't come home until nearly morning. After those "dates" she'd leave the house the next day, telling Mrs. Whiteman she was meeting a friend to do some shopping and would come home with bags from Bergdorf Goodman, Henri Bendel and Bonwit Teller. She began wearing clothes and jewelry that Mama imagined movie actressses wore. Mrs. Whiteman never asked about where they came from or how she could afford these purchases, fearful of learning the answer.

Chapter 35

A New Routine

Nearly a year went by in a rush of days and nights. The only hitch in Gigi's day was the need to spend more time with Larry who was up at 6:30 am, just a few hours after she'd gone to sleep. But she'd get up, make him breakfast, play with him until he was ready for a nap, and sink back into her bed as soon as he was tucked in. They would play and talk until she had to dress for work and he would watch her put on make-up.

Because he was almost always with adults, Larry learned to speak and understand most grownup conversation. While watching her prepare for work he would tell her "You're like a clown, Mommy" as she put on her makeup. On summer afternoons when there was no rehearsal, Gigi would take her son to the playground and when the weather turned cold they played games in the house. On rehearsal days he stayed with Mrs. Whiteman but Gigi knew he was not happy about her being away so much. Sometimes she took him along to the rehearsal hall and all the girls oohed and aahed and played with him. He would clumsily imitate their movements and the line would collapse in laughter. Gigi glowed with pride at all he knew and did. The dancemaster, however, was not pleased, so Larry did not come along often.

Chapter 36

Carroll Gardens – 78th Precinct

Detective Harley went back into the kitchen that now held only the faintest smell of gas. He stood by the broken window, and looked at the neatly planted vegetable beds in the back yard, then turned and surveyed the room. He walked around the entire kitchen. He stopped at the stove, took out his notepad and wrote about the photograph of the two dead people. They were sitting at a table in a nightclub, holding hands, she smiling into the camera, he gazing at her, adoringly. He took note of the unlit votive candle alongside the photo. If it had been lit, the house would have gone up like a bomb.

"Did you dust the gas jets for prints?" he called to the technicians who had joined the police.

"I turned them all off," Officer O'Hara said. Harley gave him a nasty look.

"Okay, I guess you had to do that," he said. "Did you touch anything else?"

"Yeah," O'Hara replied. "I picked up that chair to smash the window and then I opened the other window. Oh, and I checked their pulses in the neck. That's it."

Harley then walked to the table. There was an empty iodine bottle lying on its side. He looked at the dead man and saw a smear of iodine on his lip. He squatted down then, to look at the woman. She was very young and very beautiful. Her long black hair fanned out around her head like a large feathery headdress. On her lower jaw was a fist-sized purple bruise. Her body, spread out on the floor looked relaxed, as though on a bed.

O'Hara said, "The guy was dead but she still had some of a pulse when I got here. But when the ambulance guys came they said she was gone." I think she was really fighting to stay alive."

"From the way it looks to me," said the detective, "looks like he knocked her out and then committed suicide — with the iodine and the gas he figured he'd do both of them. I'll go talk to the grieving widow and her 'brudders,' and see what their story is. Tell the ambulance guys we're not ready for them to take the bodies yet."

He skipped down the stairs and knocked on the door.

"Whaddya want?" asked Josefina as she opened the door a few inches.

"I have to ask you and your brothers a few questions. Can I come in?"

Josefina crossed her arms over her chest. "We got nothin' to say to you. They dead, that's all, and good riddance, like they say." She seemed calm now.

"Mrs. Fiorelli, how could you come home and not smell the gas right away?" No response. "Do you have children, ma'am?" When she nodded yes, he asked where they were. As he took out his notepad and pen she began to close the door.

"Hold it, lady, this is police investigation. You can answer my questions here and now or come down to the station. Now back away so that I can come in," Harley said in a strong, stern voice.

She made a 'tsk' sound with her tongue but backed away from the door and let Harley in. They were in a kitchen, laid out like the apartment upstairs. The three brothers sat at the table, their hands clasped in front of them as though at school. Harley looked at the three men, noted that they wore workmen's clothes and seemed rough cut. By now their names had become Americanized. Luigi was Lou, Antonio was called Tony and Paolo was Pauly. They looked at the detective with blank faces, blank eyes. He knew he'd get no help here.

Chapter 37

Gerry

Gerry was finding more time to spend at home. He was getting to know his children and Josefina was pleased that he was content to be there. He still commanded a top purse and was getting a lot of fights, but he was finding it a little harder to win all his matches. He made no mention of this to Josefina but he spoke with his friends about the changes he was feeling. They told him this was to be expected and that though he handled himself more professionally, his body was paying a price.

His lovemaking was different too but Josefina had always been suspicious of his time away from home. She assumed he had women when he was out of town. He sought her body less often but as long as he came home to her when he returned to the city she put these thoughts from her mind.

Gerry, on the other hand, wondered why he desired Josefina less and less. He enjoyed the children who were growing like weeds and he loved being with them. He came home more and more, but in truth, only to be with them. He also started to wonder what he would do to earn a living when the fights ran out. All this was much on his mind and he remembered what her father had said, in what seemed to him like a hundred years ago. He did not share any of these thoughts with Josefina. He wanted her to think of him as invincible, strong forever. Until now he always had enough money to give her for the things she asked for as well as enough for his own needs but he was beginning to think about the day when the lucrative purses would be closed to him.

Chapter 38

Money Problems

Some years before when the tenants in the downstairs apartment moved out, Josefina had sent tickets to Italy for her brothers. Three of them came and moved into the empty apartment and lived there rent-free. It annoyed him that he didn't have a rent-paying tenant to help out, now that he was concerned about money. When he mentioned asking her brothers for rent, it was the first time he had seen his wife totally furious.

"You have money for everything you want – your car, your clothes, your whores – and you want to bleed my brothers to pay for that," she screamed. "Never!" She turned and walked away from him. He was shocked by her outburst at the simple request. That was the moment Gerry realized how much she had changed. It was also the moment he lost all feeling for Josefina. On her part, her anger and pride were stronger than her own needs and desires. She felt that her brothers were the only people she could count on and vowed that never again would she allow Gerry to touch her.

Gerry came home most nights, to have dinner and see the children. Josefina had learned since childhood that a wife must provide a clean home and meals for her husband. She felt she owed Gerry nothing more. In time he came home less and less. She never asked where he had been, pretending not to care, too proud to show any interest in his life. She turned to her brothers for companionship and spent her days with her son and daughter, attending to their needs and desires. As they grew older, she lived vicariously through their accomplishments

Lillian Lee Liss

and activities. They filled her days and her life. She listened as they did homework, heard about the friends they spent time with, even went to the homes of those friends to assure herself that they were "nice." Less time was spent with her neighbors since she didn't want to answer their questions, nor did her pride allow her to share her heartache with people who, in the end, were strangers.

Chapter 39

Finding Gigi

Gerry, when he felt the need for a woman, had no problem finding a willing partner ready to pleasure him. He hit the local clubs, much as he had before his marriage. It was on one of these nights that he saw Gigi. Most nights he hardly noticed the women who danced in the chorus. That night, Gigi was studiously concentrating on the dance number, with her professional smile pasted on. She started to giggle at something Bunny whispered to her. At that moment, Gerry caught her eye and he began to laugh too. This caused her to giggle harder and she had to turn away to stop, which put her head in the wrong position for the dance. It took only a few seconds to make things right but when the girls left the stage Gerry went backstage to look for Gigi. The girlish giggle had made him laugh, something missing from his life for quite a while.

He was not allowed into the dressing room and was told to wait near the stage door. When Gigi came out she was surprised to see him standing in the tight backstage area. He came right to her and asked her to have a drink with him. She refused.

"Sorry, I have to get home," she told him.

"I'll take you home," he countered.

"No thanks, I'm leaving with my friend," she pointed to Bunny. "She depends on me to keep her company. See ya," she waved airily. She left with Bunny, leaving Gerry surprised and disappointed.

He came to the club every night that week and offered to take her home. Each night she refused. She wasn't particularly attracted to the man even though he was handsome and she didn't like the look of the people he came in with. He, on the other hand, couldn't get her off his mind. She grew more beautiful to him each night, more so with each refusal. At the end of the week, when this show ended, he worried that he would have no idea where to find her.

The last night she was to be at the club he waited backstage with a large, shiny white box tied with a gold bow. He took her elbow when she came out of the dressing room and led her to a corner.

"This is for you," he said with a slight accent. "I can't stop thinking about you. I want to see you, to spend some time with you. Please don't say no. If you don't like me after you get to know me, I'll go away. Give me a chance. Please."

She had learned how to turn away stubborn suitors before. But his pleas, softly spoken with his accent somewhat stronger than usual because he was anxious, sounded sincere and persuasive.

Gigi decided she would keep things light. "What did you get me," she asked coyly.

"Look," he said. He held the box while she pulled the bow open and took the top off. She opened the tissue and saw fur. She looked up at him and said, "What is it?"

He lifted the garment out – a long, pale lynx coat – and slipped it around her shoulders. He lifted her long hair, now dyed jet black, out of the coat.

"You make it look good," he said. His eyes devoured her face and he would have grabbed her, held her close if he could. Gigi was stunned. She'd received expensive gifts from many of the men she had dated since she'd started working the clubs, but nothing quite so sumptuous or valuable as this fur.

"I don't think I can take this. It's very beautiful and I thank you for thinking about me, but this is too much. I don't even know you. What's your name?" She saw the hunger in his eyes and backed away, taking the coat from her shoulders and handing it back to him.

Chapter 40

Another Beginning

"My name is Gerry," he said. He started to pour out his heart. "You and I were fated to be together to the end. I know it and you will too. Don't be afraid. I will be there for you, to take care of you. Nothing can stop this. If not tonight then another time. We belong to each other."

She waited for Bunny and was relieved to get into a cab and head for home. Gigi had been frightened by the intensity of his look, by the force of his words.

Thereafter, he seemed to know every night of the dancers' engagements, the clubs they played. Gerry was always there at a ringside table, some nights for the early show, sometimes the late show. Some nights he had bruises on his face. After each show he invited Gigi to have a drink with him. She came, but always with Bunny or one of the other girls. He knew this was deliberate but accepted the situation so that she would sit with him. One week, after one of the shows finished, Gigi knew he was following the cab that took her home.

Chapter 41

A Changing World

When Gigi came out the next morning, wheeling baby Larry in his stroller, she was shocked to see Gerry still in his car, parked at the curb.

He got out of the car and walked over to her. "You are married? This is your child?" he asked.

"What are you doing here?" Gigi responded. When he didn't answer she began walking away. He called after her and asked again, "Are you married?"

She half-turned and said, "Separated. And yes, this is my son. Now you tell me what you're doing here."

Gerry thought about what she had said. "What do you mean, separated," he asked. He began walking alongside her.

"It means that my husband and I no longer live together. We'll probably get divorced. Our lives go different ways. You still didn't tell me what you're doing here. What do you want?"

"What do I want," Gerry repeated, as he walked along beside her. "I want you. I want to be with you, maybe for all times. I love you. You are the most beautiful woman I have ever seen. Don't think I say this lightly. I don't want you to ever be with another man, just with me. Maybe you need time to get used to me. I will give you that time. But you must never go with anyone else. I will always be here."

"Listen," said Gigi, "I don't even know you and you really don't know me. This is silly. You can't tell me what to do and how to live my life. I'm finished with that kind of man. Maybe you better leave now. You're making me nervous."

He stopped her by putting his arm around her shoulder and pulling her close to him. "You don't ever have to be nervous with me," he said. I'll be here tonight to take you to work. We will be two hearts beating together like one. I will see you later." With that, he turned and walked back to his car. Gigi caught her breath and began to walk the carriage to the playground without even thinking of her destination. She didn't know whether to be afraid or to laugh, but fear won.

Their affair, their relationship, began that night. Gigi felt powerless to stop Gerry's pursuit. He was parked in front of the house when she came down to go to work. He got out of the car to open the door for her and held her elbow to help her in. They rode in silence. When they reached the club where she was to work, he repeated the whole performance, opened the door and took her hand to help her out of the car.

Chapter 42

The Affair

"Wait," he said, "stand here." He went to the trunk and took the lynx coat out of the box and slipped it over her shoulders. He lifted her hair over the collar and walked her to the stage door. She felt as though she were in a dream and could not wake up. He opened the door and she went inside, alone.

Once inside, she leaned against the wall to steady herself and then went into the dressing room. Some of the other dancers had already started putting on their makeup and were in various states of undress. Costumes hung from pegs on the wall. They were doing five numbers that night and there were five different sets of costumes. No one turned when Gigi came in until one of the women noticed the coat.

"Wow, honey, you had a good night!" she exclaimed. Then all of them turned to admire the beautiful garment. Gigi was a bit embarrassed by the attention.

"I tried to give it back, but he wouldn't take no for an answer," she said.

"Are you crazy? That's a killer coat, said the woman who had first noticed. "Don't you know you never say no to a gift? I guess that's one lesson Bunny never taught you, huh? Enjoy it, Babe. I'm sure you'll find a way to say thanks." The others nodded and laughed along with her.

Gerry was at ringside when she came out on stage. He was alone, which was unusual for him. She'd told Bunny and Mary Russell, another old friend from the Bronx luncheonette crowd, what had happened and that she was uncomfortable about this man's intensity.

"Don't worry. Once he gets what he wants he'll be out of the picture. You know how they are – make him happy and he'll disappear," said Mary. If prior experience counted, that's exactly how it had been with other "dates" although several men had continued to see her for a relatively long time until they quietly faded from sight. Gigi didn't want any long-term relationships at this point in her life. The short romances suited her. More would have added complications and that's what she feared from Gerry. She didn't even know why she felt that he would not leave a relationship easily but the thought troubled her.

At the end of the show, she got dressed and knew he was waiting for her to join him. She asked Bunny and Mary to come with her. They sat at the table and after everyone had ordered a drink, Gerry looked at Gigi and told her it was time to go.

Bunny said, "I was planning to go home with Gigi. Will you give me a ride too?"

"Are you ready to leave now?" Gerry asked without taking his eyes away from Gigi. Bunny nodded yes. They left and Gerry drove Bunny to her door. Then he and Gigi drove away.

Chapter 43

Lovers

He didn't stop or speak until they reached a deserted commercial street near the waterfront. When he stopped the car he moved to her side. He took her face in his two hands and brought his lips to hers. He kissed her long and passionately. Her response was cool. She knew he expected to make love to her but between fear of him and anger at having nothing to say in the matter, she felt no return of his ardor.

"You are not ready for me, are you?" he asked.

"You didn't ask me if I wanted to be here with you," she replied, fury clear in her voice. "I didn't want your fur and now you expect me to pay for it, don't you?"

He had never been turned down by any other woman before and was a bit shocked by her anger.

"No, no, I gave you the coat to show you my love. It's not payment for anything. I meant no insult. Please, I haven't felt such love in a very long time. I just want to be near you, to hold you if nothing else. Don't think I mean disrespect. Don't be angry."

He continued to tell her his feelings. His voice was soft, urgent. He stroked her hair, ran his fingers along her face while he spoke. As she listened she began to warm, sensing more than just the words but also the import of his desire. His ardor awakened an unfamiliar response in her.

She thought back to Gary, her long-absent husband, whom she once thought she loved. He had never had this kind of patience with her and his lovemaking was perfunctory – over almost before it began. There was no stroking, no speaking, no coaxing. Gigi was being aroused by the sound of this man's voice, his urgency and his gentle touch.

When he reached to kiss her again he could feel softness where before she was taut and restrained. He pressed on and soon they were entwined. It was uncomfortable in the car but they managed to find ways to explore each other's body. Soon they were both panting and in moments Gerry had removed her tiny bikini panties and she straddled him and so they made love. It was the first time she had ever reached orgasm and Gigi was overwhelmed. She rested her spent body on his and he was content to feel the weight of her on him. It was everything he had hoped for.

Thereafter he waited for her every working day that he was not fighting. After the night's work was over they went to one of the elegant hotels in downtown Brooklyn where he reserved a room on a permanent basis. Each time they stayed a bit longer until Gigi was not coming home until nearly morning on the nights she was with Gerry. He could not get enough of her body and her warmth, now that she was returning his passion in full measure. She loved his Italian murmurings, love words that she began to recognize. He hated to end the night but she insisted that she must go home to take care of little Larry.

Chapter 44

New Arrangements

Gigi's marriage no longer existed except as a legality. She never saw Gary anymore. He had moved to California, "to the coast," as he wrote her, where he had found jobs arranging music for many well-known performers. It turned out that his talent was in writing and arranging and he had lots of steady work. He no longer asked about the little guy in the song he had written that had helped to establish his reputation. In time, both Gigi and Larry were forgotten by their short-term husband and father.

Josefina, too, no longer had a marriage. Gerry did go to his home when he was not with Gigi, but barely spoke a word to his wife. He still enjoyed his children but they were beginning to feel his absence and their mother did nothing to make them less resentful. He was not the kind of father who played with them or took them to museums, to ball games or shows, things he had never known. He came into the house as a visitor. She could feel that something different was happening. Josefina understood that a man could have many women and still need his wife, but if there was just one other woman in his life, the wife was finished. She could sense that this was so now.

Chapter 45

Carroll Gardens – 78th Precinct

The investigation of the apartment was in full swing. Technicians were dusting for prints, the medical examiner came to give the official pronouncement of death. Detective Harley meanwhile was struggling with the wife and family, attempting to get some information – any information. It was slow going and he was meeting resistance with every question. More and more he was beginning to feel they had much to cover up. Something definitely did not smell right and it wasn't the gas fumes that still lingered.

Chapter 46

Gerry and Gigi

Gerry began taking Gigi all over with him on nights when she was not working. When she watched him fight, sitting at ringside, she cried when he was punched and clutched her heart at the pain he must be feeling. Afterward they went out and made the rounds of after-hours clubs and when they were alone she kissed the bruises and the cuts. Friends knew them as an item and none had ever seen him so enamored before.

The heat of their love continued to burn for more than the six months that Mrs. Whiteman had considered the limit. There was no inch of her body that was stranger to his lips, his tongue and fingers. One night, as they were making love, as Gerry fondled and licked Gigi's breasts he noticed that they were fuller and rounder. And she had a bit of a belly, which had always been flat and hard from the dancing.

"You're getting fat, cara mia. Better watch your diet or you won't fit into your costumes," he teased. "But there's more for me to enjoy. I love you so much, there could never be enough."

Gigi sat up and pulled him up beside her. "I'm pregnant, my love. You're going to be a father," she told him in a shaky voice.

The news caught him by surprise. He knew that not only was it possible but probable, yet he was surprised. He didn't know how he felt about her pregnancy. In his mind there was only her. She filled his life.

Gerry saw her looking at his face, trying to read his reaction.

"That's wonderful, my love," he said. I am one with you and now there will be always something that is of both of us." Gigi let out a breath and relaxed.

Chapter 47

Carroll Gardens – 78th Precinct

Detective Harley knew he was going to have a hard time trying to learn anything from these people. He looked around at the brothers' kitchen and could tell that no woman shared these premises. There was nothing that could be construed as decoration. Stacks of clean dishes stood on the counter, dirty ones were piled in the sink, worn dishtowels hung from the oven handles, no cloth graced the table, the chairs did not match and the stove needed a good cleaning. Only shades covered the windows, no curtains. He looked at the brothers sitting at the table, they looked back but said nothing.

"Were you home all day? " he asked them. No answer.

"Dey no speaka da English," Josefina said flatly. Harley called to one of the officers still in the upstairs apartment. "Valente, you talk Italian?" he yelled up the steps. He pronounced the I in Italian as eye. Valente came down the stairs and was enlisted in the questioning.

"They say they were home all day," Valente translated.

"Didn't you hear people coming in and going upstairs?" he wanted to know. The brothers nodded yes. "Weren't you curious about who had come in, about the noises?" he asked.

"No," they replied, "we thought it was Gerry and Josi. That maybe they were arguing."

"What about when Mrs. Fiorelli came home, didn't that make you think someone who didn't belong was up there?" Harley asked. They shrugged, collectively.

"When did you smell gas?" Harley asked. More shrugs. "Mrs. Fiorelli, when you came in, didn't you smell gas?" the detective wanted to know. Didn't your brothers tell you someone was in your house and that you should go up and check on what was happening?

"I didn' pay attenshun," she responded.

"When do you expect your children home?"

"My kids is wit dere friends." The detective knew he'd get no information here. He went back up the steps to re-examine the room.

He took out his notepad and wrote about the bruise on the woman's jaw, the empty bottle of iodine, the rags stuffed around the windows and the door. Harley continued to walk around the apartment, noting that it was clean, there were religious pictures on the walls and lots of artificial flowers in cheap glass vases. The children's rooms held evidence of their interests, the boy's room had athletic equipment and books, the girl's, dolls, records and books.

He gave the ambulance people permission to take the bodies to the morgue. Back in the kitchen he took the lynx coat from the back of a chair, a handbag from the floor, and with a paper napkin, picked up the iodine bottle from the table. Then he took the votive candle that had been placed near the picture on the stove, but not lit, as well as the photo. The towels and rags that had blocked the door and windows were examined. The photo, the candle, the iodine bottle, the fur coat and handbag were bundled up in a towel and taken for further study. Finally, the two bodies were placed on gurneys and taken to the waiting ambulance.

Chapter 48

Neighbors

The Fiorelli children returned home in time to see the sheet-covered bodies rolling out of the building and loaded into an ambulance. They ran into the house, terrified and frantic. Their mother met them in the hallway and pulled them into the house and shut the door. Neighbors standing around the street were buzzing, asking the police what had happened.

"A gas leak," Officer O'Hara said.

"Who died," they wanted to know. "Mr. Fiorelli and a friend," he advised. At that, mouths clamped shut and some of the people started to walk back to their homes.

Chapter 49

Gigi and Gerry in Suburbia

Days after he learned she was pregnant, Gerry told Gigi he had bought a house for them in the suburbs, in Spring Valley. He said she would stop working and move in and raise his family there. Gigi told her mother everything. She told her mother about her pregnancy, which Mama Whiteman already suspected, and about moving to a house of her own. Mama did not think this was a good idea and told her not to go. Ignoring her mother's advice, Gigi packed her belongings and Larry's clothes and toys into a few cartons and valises. She told the child that from now on they would have lots of time together. She brought him along when she met Gerry that afternoon, so that they could get to know one another. The little boy, now three and a half years old, was a bit frightened of this stranger and clung to his mother. At first this made Gerry laugh but then he became annoyed, even angry at the child's close attachment to his mother.

When they came home from their outing Papa Whiteman was waiting for them in the kitchen.

"Do you know what you are doing," he raged. His angry questions poured out and over her. "Do you know this man? What kind of person is he, he already has a wife and a family. What does that make you? How will you raise your son? This is not a good thing. If you move out you will be like a lost person and not know where you belong. Who knows if we will ever see you again. The man is a violent person, a fighter. Think more before you do this," Papa cautioned.

Many of the doubts Gigi had in her own mind echoed through

her father's tirade. She knew he spoke more in anguish than anger. But just as she couldn't admit that marrying Gary had been a mistake, she stubbornly would not give her father the satisfaction of admitting he was right in this instance. She was making a move that left her both sad and excited. In any case, things had gone too far, she was carrying Gerry's child and needed him to support her growing family. In a few days she was out of the Whiteman house and into the home Gerry had bought in Spring Valley.

Chapter 50

Spring Valley

It was foreign territory to her, Spring Valley. There were no neighborhood stores within walking distance. She could not drive nor did she have a car. If she needed milk, bread or other necessities she had to wait for Gerry to return home and take her shopping. It was a new development and she knew no one on the block.

The house was newly built and empty when he bought it, and was still barely furnished since they had not had an opportunity to shop for such things as curtains or rugs. Window shades, bought hastily, provided privacy. The wood floors were bare. They'd bought sets of furniture for the bedroom and kitchen that could be delivered in a few days, and some sheets and towels, pillows and blankets. The living room held only a sofa and a radio. Larry's room had a bed and a dresser brought over from the Whiteman house in the trunk and back of Gerry's Cadillac. Only enough linens to carry through to washday sat in the near-empty linen closet. She promised herself that while waiting for the baby to be born she would spend days shopping to make the house a home. But she had no way of getting to the shops and the house had the look of a temporary shelter. She shopped for necessities when Gerry came. The opportunity to shop for household furniture and accessories never came since there was no one to take her to the stores.

The trip up to Spring Valley was farther from the city than Gerry realized. It was not like driving from Manhattan to Brooklyn, and he found himself spending many fight nights in the Brooklyn apartment. On those nights Gigi was alone with only the little boy for company.

When it was nearly time for her to give birth she found that she had grown clumsy and was fearful of being by herself. She told Gerry she wanted to stay at her mother's house until the baby was born, especially since she was due to give birth at a hospital in Brooklyn. He agreed.

Gigi was happier at the Whiteman's home during the three weeks she spent there before giving birth than the few months in Spring Valley, where she had not made a single friend. She went shopping with her mother, who had accepted her condition in her usual practical manner. They had a wonderful time buying furniture and accessories for the house, to be delivered when she returned home. She piled curtains, sheets, towels and more blankets into cartons. Cookies, candy, other treats and staples went into another carton to bring back with her. She ordered a crib and all the complementary furniture for a nursery, also to be delivered after the baby was born. Gerry paid all the bills. Her mother approved.

She gave birth to a beautiful girl on a cool fall day. Gigi named the baby Jerrilyn, telling Gerry she had been named for him. He was delighted. Gigi spent two weeks at her mother's home after leaving the hospital, to get her strength back, she told Gerry. When they returned to Spring Valley she felt a pang of regret at leaving her mother. Larry cried at leaving the warmth of his grandparent's home. As she comforted the little boy, Gigi would have cried too, if she could have articulated a reason for tears.

Once back in the suburban house Gigi threw herself into housekeeping. She now had a phone that worked, she hung curtains, ordered the newspaper delivered, found ads in the local press for storekeepers who would bring almost everything she needed to the door. Diapers and formula were delivered too. She insisted that Gerry take her to the stores. She bought lamps and area rugs, vases for flowers, pictures to hang on the walls. The house was spotlessly clean and neat, even with an infant and a toddler in residence. Cleaning became an outlet for her restlessness.

Chapter 51

Housekeeping

The two children kept her busy. Walks around the neighborhood were primarily to provide fresh air to the children but in time some of the neighbors began to smile and then to wave at the young mother. She dieted and exercised strenuously and worked at getting herself back in shape. Larry exercised along with her and made her laugh. As the house brightened, Gigi took more of an interest in how she looked, and paid more attention to her grooming. Gerry began making the trip to Spring Valley on every night that he did not have a fight scheduled.

Within a month they began making love again. Gigi asked Gerry to take precautions to prevent another pregnancy, something he had never done before. He agreed but just for a while, he told her. He loved the look of the house and even began to plant flowers and a sapling apple tree. Playing with the earth appealed to him and took him back to another, earlier time and place. This house became more a home to him than any other. He began to follow his customary routines, starting the day with setting up exercises. Before breakfast he made himself a concoction of marsala wine and raw eggs. He said this made him strong and virile. Gigi had her morning coffee with him but ate nothing else until Gerry came home for dinner. She restricted her diet to steak and salad until she reached her old weight. Their life took on a domestic rhythm that suited both of them.

Chapter 52

The Italian Grandmother's House -- Brooklyn

Gerry's mother, Concetta, was growing old and a bit fragile. He visited her for a little while every day that he was in the city. Gerry had not told her he was no longer living with Josefina nor that he had another woman, another child, another home. He knew she would not approve. However, Josefina made a rare visit to her mother-in-law and told her of her suspicions. The old woman said nothing to Josefina, but stored the information, readying it for the next visit of her son.

He came a day later. He had no idea that Josefina had been to see his mother, so when he sat down at her table with his cup of coffee and a pastry, he was unprepared for her words.

"Are you a sinner, my son? Are you no longer a husband to your lawful wife, or a father to your God-given Italian children? Her voice sounded like the voice of doom. You will pay a bitter price if you are doing this to your family," she intoned.

"Mama, what are you saying, what are you talking about," he asked nervously. Who is telling you such things? He was not particularly religious but he had no wish to hurt or offend his mother. He flushed red with guilt.

"I know when you lie to me, my son. No good will come of this. Can you give this woman up? Can you go back to a righteous life?" she asked.

He hung his head, then answered. "No mama, I can't. I love this woman more than my life. She is the mother of my child too. Josefina stopped being a wife to me a long time ago. I know this is wrong but I am powerless to stop it. I'm sorry if I hurt my other children and I'm sorry if you are disappointed in me."

His mother had always cared more about what he felt than about what society and the world decided what was right or wrong. Once again she saw the tormented boy of years before.

"Giovanni, I can forgive you anything, but you should pray that God will be forgiving. I wish you peace in your heart," said his mother. "What will you tell your children when they grow up," she asked. Gerry shook his head from side to side.

"I can only take care of one day at a time now," he answered. But having his mother know what was happening in his life suddenly made his mind and heart easier.

Chapter 53

Home – Where the Heart Is

He went back to Spring Valley that afternoon with a box of Italian pastry from the famous Ferrara bakery, in a festive mood. When he got home, the house was empty and he was disappointed. After an hour, Gigi came down the block, laughing and playing with Larry, wheeling the baby in her carriage. His heart both lifted and fell at the sight. Gigi looked more beautiful than ever and he would have taken her to bed as she stepped into the house but knew he could not with the children there. He loved the infant girl who had been named for him but found that he resented the little boy who was a stranger to him. He was in the way and was a constant reminder of the father who had been Gigi's first partner. The child sensed his distaste and instinctively hid behind his mother as they went into the house.

In time Gigi saw that the more time Gerry spent at home with them, the less her son flourished. Gerry never touched the child but there was bad feeling between them. She tried to bring them together but did not succeed.

"I can't look at him without knowing you loved someone else," Gerry told her. She began to fear for the boy's well-being. One day she asked Larry, "Would you like to stay at grandma's house for a while?"

"Will you come too," he asked. She told him no, that she must remain here. The boy, sensing the tension in the house when Gerry was there, agreed to stay with his grandparents for a little while. After he left Gigi missed him terribly. Although the baby girl provided pleasure and took up much of her time, Larry was her company through the day while Gerry was away. With the child gone the house seemed emptier, lonelier.

Chapter 54

What Happened Here?

Gerry was going to be away for several days. He was booked for two fights on the West Coast. They went marketing and bought enough food and supplies to last until he returned home. After three days, Gigi, alone with the baby and no one to talk to, got cabin fever and needed to get out. That night, after she put the baby to bed, she decided to walk the mile to the movie theater in town. She would be gone for no more than two, three hours and the baby always slept well for that time. A bit guiltily, she went off to the movie, but knew she needed the diversion to save her sanity.

When she got home she was surprised to see Gerry standing on the small stoop that led to the house. She was delighted to see him and was surprised when he greeted her with anger.

"Where were you?" he demanded to know. "Who were you with?" Gerry had been waiting for her to return for over an hour. He'd been envisioning her in someone else's arms, so that by the time she came home he was sure she was coming from an assignation. "Is this what you do when I am not here?"

Gigi was confused by his vehemence. "What are you talking about," she asked. "I was at the movies…" Before she could say any more he ran down the steps and landed a blow to her head. Once started, he began to beat her, tearing at her clothes as she tried to elude him, until she stood nearly naked, bleeding, cowering, until she fell to the ground. Only then did he stop the onslaught.

A neighbor who had looked out the window at the sound of the argument had called the police when he started beating Gigi. When the police car pulled up they saw a nearly naked woman, reeling as she tried to walk. They took a blanket from the car, wrapped it around her and one of the officers took her to the emergency room of the nearest hospital. The other officer went into the house where he found a man, sitting in the living room, elbows on knees, holding his head in hands.

"What happened here," he asked. Jerry merely shook his head and shrugged.

"Where's Gigi," Jerry wanted to know.

"That your wife?" the officer asked. He nodded yes.

"Did you beat her up?" He gave no answer. "She's at Garden Hill Hospital," the policeman told him. To the cops this was just another domestic dispute. When his partner returned, they left. Gerry went to the hospital and asked to see Gigi. They led him into a room. Gigi's face was swollen to nearly double its size and covered with scratches and blotches that were turning blue and purple. Her arms, with which she had tried to fend him off, were similarly marked, as was her body, which was covered with a sheet. A nurse came in and glared at Gerry.

"She's in bad shape. She doesn't know her name or where she is. Whoever did this to her should be in jail," the middle-aged woman said.

"You right," said Gerry, his accent coming out. He stood at the bedside, tears running down his face. He reached out to stroke her hair but the nurse gave a curt order, "Don't touch her!" He turned to the nurse with a questioning look on his face.

"She's badly damaged. Every touch causes her pain," the nurse said in hard voice. "It's best if she's left alone. She needs time to heal."

Gerry went back to the house. He wrapped the sleeping baby in a few blankets, put the carriage into his car and put the baby into the carriage. He drove to Brooklyn and dropped the baby at the Whiteman's home. He told them Gigi had had an accident and was in the hospital. Then he left and went to Josefina's house.

Chapter 55

Family Support

The following days were difficult and busy days for the Whiteman family. Mrs. Whiteman had to stay with the children but the five sisters went upstate to the hospital to find out what had happened to Gigi. They were stunned by the sight of her . She had trouble remembering their names or anything that had happened. Each of them took a turn staying at her side.

She went home to her mother's house. Most of the time she spent with the children but every evening Jerry came to see how she was faring. He brought flowers and gifts. The Whitemans were not happy about his visits but could think of no way to stop them. Gigi was pleased when he came. She had no memory of the beating. Her recovery was slow but her mother's loving care helped her heal.

One evening, Jerry came and said he had good news. Josefina told him she was willing to discuss a divorce. She asked him to bring his paramour, not the word she used, to the house the next morning after the children left for school to discuss terms.

Chapter 56

Carroll Gardens – 78th Precinct

Detective Harley took his collection of the "evidence" wrapped in the towel as he got ready to go back to the station house. He had told the widow she could go back into her apartment. The window had to be fixed, the place cleaned up and he felt there was no more he could gain from further examination. Her brothers, his "witnesses," had nothing to tell him and their fingerprints, all over the apartment, had legitimate reasons for being present.

He asked the children where they'd been and they told him, "With friends." He asked if they usually went to the home of friends after school and they said, "Sometimes." Even they were closed-mouth and wary of the strange man.

The few neighbors who were still standing around the stoop asked Detective Harley about what had happened.

"There's been some trouble here. Do you know if the Flowers' were having problems," Harley asked. At that, several of the women passed knowing looks among each other but answered that they knew nothing.

"Who's the dead friend," they wanted to know and he told them that Gerry Flowers and a friend of his had died from a gas leak.

"Uh huh," said one of the women sarcastically, " a gas leak. Okay." They began to break up, going in different directions. Harley knew they didn't believe that explanation any more than he did. Officer O'Hara, who had been standing near the curb writing in his little notepad, had heard the women talking before the detective came out. One had said, "I knew it would end like this. Those brothers believe in vendetta, they're from the old country."

The captain of the local precinct, who had come to the crime scene, had been standing at the side of the house with Officer O'Hara and now with Detective

Harley, took in the scene. "You're right. Something's not right here," he said. Harley agreed but said he had nothing to go on to justify going further.

When they returned to the station house the captain, whose name was George Von Holsten, asked to see the evidence collected by Detective Harley. He had heard about the arrogance of the wife, the lack of sorrow and felt there was surely more to this than what had so far been heard or seen. The captain, called Dutch by his men, was all spit and polish. New recruits thought he was a hardass but the old-timers who had been in the station with him for years had respect for his ability and his regard for the law. He had solved many cases that others had missed or overlooked, mostly by his tenacity and perseverance. He decided to visit the grieving widow the next morning and see what he could learn.

When he arrived at the apartment Josefina was just returning from taking the children to school and nursery school. The boy was 6, the girl 4. They were at an age when the world revolved around their own needs. Their father had spent little of the last few years with them for any length of time, so they mourned him fleetingly, as they would a kind uncle. Captain Von Holsten tromped up the steps just behind Josefina .

Chapter 57

A New Chapter

Von Holsten introduced himself, showed his badge and asked if he might come in to ask a few questions. He was surprised to see that Josefina was not outfitted in black as was customary in this neighborhood for the Italian women who became widows. Perhaps it was too early in the day for black, he thought.

This lady was wearing the flowered housedress and cardigan that was the uniform of the day in the neighborhood, unless or until it was time to dress when one went out for a social occasion. Her brown hair, now streaked with a few strands of gray, was pulled back and knotted into a bun at the nape of her neck. Stray tendrils curled around her face. The vee-neck of her housedress revealed a generous amount of cleavage between her ample breasts. The captain didn't realize he was staring. He thought her quite attractive.

"What you want?" Josefina asked. Her question snapped Captain Von Holsten back to the reason he had come.

"It seems strange to me, Signora," he said, "that you would come home, know there were people in your apartment, smell gas, and still sit and chat with your brothers without going up to see what was happening. Weren't you curious? What were these people doing in your house. Did you know who was there? Obviously, you and your husband were not getting along, but here he was with the woman who was – pardon me for saying this, – taking your place. And again, what were they doing here?"

Josefina sat down in one of the kitchen chairs, crooked her elbow on the table, leaned her head on her hand and looked Von Holsten in the eyes. "I don't know -- and no one can ask them, can they? If you think I will make believe that I care, I tell you, I don't. I'm glad they are dead. That's all I can say."

"Did you and your brothers kill them," he asked just as bluntly. She smiled, shook her head from side to side and then shrugged.

"You got any more questions," she asked. He looked at her, aware that she was dismissing him. He was intrigued. This was one cool customer, he thought. No, not cool, cold. But honest.

Chapter 58

"Will you come down to the station house to identify some things," he asked. He realized that he had said this because he wanted to keep talking to her.

"When," she asked. He asked if that moment was convenient and she agreed. They went down to his car. He opened the door for her and she stepped in. They hardly spoke on the way but Von Holsten was very conscious of her presence next to him. She seemed unaware of his proximity.

At the station house he ushered her into his office and brought in the towel in which the detective had bundled the objects found in Josefina's apartment. She started, the first show of emotion, when he laid the items out on the towel on his desk. She got up and went over to look at the objects but touched nothing. She stared at the photo of Gerry and Gigi, he staring at her adoringly, she looking glamorous. A tear ran down her face but she wiped at it angrily.

"I don't know about any of this. And you can throw the towel out when you are done with it," she snapped. Von Holsten came over to her and asked softly if she would like a cup of coffee.

"I don't want anything here. Take me home," she commanded. Von Holsten found himself getting up to do her bidding. They got back into the car and on the way he suggested that they stop for coffee at a coffee shop. She agreed, glad for the company, the change of scene.

Over coffee he commiserated with her about changes in the community, spoke about his children, told her he had lost his wife two years before to cancer. She found herself enjoying a normal conversation with another adult and had almost forgotten why he had originally come to speak with her. They had spent close to an hour at the coffee shop.

"I have to go home," she said. He looked at his watch and was surprised at the passage of time. As he drove her home he asked if he could take her to a movie sometime. She thought about it, realized there was no reason she could not go. But it was too soon. People would talk. She agreed to meet him at a movie house in Manhattan a week later.

Chapter 59

Josefina and the Captain

The day before their "date" she searched for a dress that still fit and looked well, and rooted around the bottom of a closet until she found shoes with a high heel. The next morning, after the children left for the nursery and school she put rollers in her hair and when it was time to dress, she put on a bit of makeup and brushed out her hair. She had told the children she was going to see a lawyer about some legal business. She told her son to pick up his sister and bring her home. If Mama was late coming home, " she told them, "they should just do their homework or play until she got there."

She got to the theater and found Von Holsten waiting for her. He was not in uniform but was wearing slacks, a sport coat and a tie. He looked – well -- nice, she thought. Josefina didn't think of this as a real date, at first. Then it occurred to her that that's exactly what it was, and the thought pleased her. In the movie house they watched a film she might never have gone to see, but as soon as the policeman put his arm around the back of her seat she lost track of what she was seeing anyway. He wrapped his large hand around her upper arm and took the hand that rested on the arm of the seat into his.

Fast worker, she thought, but felt a pleasant tingle at his touch. He didn't know how hungry he was for the touch of another person. Neither did she until his hand was on hers. She had not had a touch or a hug from anyone but her children for several years and did not realize how strong a sexual craving she had been repressing since the last time Gerry was in bed with her. In a while he leaned over and kissed her cheek. She turned to him, meaning to ask what he was doing but instead he kissed her on the mouth, pulling her close to his chest. Hardly realizing how she was responding, she opened her mouth to his tongue and was soon lost in a melt of sensation that she felt in the pit of her stomach. His hand moved under her arm to cover her breast and they were both suddenly breathing heavily.

"Let's get out of here," he whispered. She followed him to his car and they drove to a street of deserted warehouses near the waterfront. He moved to her and began kissing again. She was as starved as he was for love and loving, and responded with the warmth she had buried, pushed inside for the last few years. He lifted her onto his lap, raised her dress and when he entered her she used her muscles to hold onto the good feeling she had been missing for so long. He could not believe the wonderful reaction he had let loose.

When it was over he told her again and again, how wonderful she was and she murmured the same to him. She had recently turned twenty-seven and was feeling the demands of her sexuality. A few years of denial had sharpened her desire beyond the ability to now consider consequences. Coming upon the right person at the right time had brought them to a juncture neither had expected or anticipated.

"It's been so long and it is so good, the policeman crooned to her. She rested her head against his shoulder, sated.

Chapter 60

Funerals

The medical examiner received Gerry's body. The autopsy showed death by gas asphyxiation. Once the decision for cause of death was made the doctor searched no further so the blow to the head was never discovered. The cadaver was released to his grieving mother for burial.

Gigi's body had gone directly to an undertaker since the Jewish religion did not permit autopsies. Mr. Whiteman had been adamant about not allowing such an examination to take place. The authorities acceded to his wishes. They agreed that the cause of death was also asphyxiation from gas inhalation – with no consideration for the bruise on her jaw.

The next day's Daily News had a small blurb on the sports page that said "Murder-Suicide Pact in Brooklyn." The article said that "boxer Gerry Flowers had killed his lover and then himself in his estranged wife's apartment." An inquest was ordered by the district attorney to take place within thirty days.

After a review of the facts and the coroner's report, the inquest found that the pair, out of guilt, had made a suicide pact. They said that the man had then knocked the woman out so that she would not change her mind. Despite a mountain of evidence, including motive, means and opportunity, they could not come up with a reason to call the event a double murder. Although they did question why this had taken place in the home of the betrayed wife they based their conclusion on the police report and a recommendation from the captain of the local precinct that corroborated the medical examiner's findings. The case was closed.

Josefina, showing renewed confidence, and displaying some her old arrogance, attended the inquest with her brothers. The five remaining Whiteman sisters were also present. As all the participants were leaving the municipal building when the inquest was over, the youngest Whiteman sister approached Josefina.

"You killed my sister," she accused. "She loved life and would never commit suicide. You are a murderer and someday that will be proven and you will pay the price," she said with a sob.

Josefina turned to her and with a wicked smile replied, "If you think so, why don't you go down to hell and ask her?" With a toss of her head she strutted out, her brothers trailing behind.

In the taxi going home, her brothers heard Josefina, feeling triumphant, mutter again and again, "It's over."

Chapter 61

More Questions

Another person not happy with this verdict was Detective Harley. He came into the Captain's office and plunked down into a chair. Von Holsten looked at him enquiringly, an eyebrow raised.

"There's no way this is as cut and dried as they say it is," the detective said. "Those people, that woman and her brothers, had plenty to do with this. Do we just let them get away with it?"

Von Holsten shrugged. "You were not going to get any more out of anyone than you have already. Drop it and we'll call the case closed." Harley's mouth dropped open, shocked by this uncharacteristic response. Von Holsten, looking directly at Harley, said again, "Drop it, okay." Harley understood there was more here than he needed to know. "Politics," he mumbled, shook his head and walked out of the office.

Chapter 62

A Different Affair

Josefina kept her relationship with Captain Von Holsten secret. He had told her that she would never have to worry about the strange deaths in her home. The case was closed and he had sent the documentation to the archives.

He vowed he would take care of her and as she continued to see him, she allowed herself to indulge all of her long-repressed desires in his bed. He marveled at her hunger and enjoyed the fruits of her needy body. Together they explored their new-found sensuality. Always, however, she returned to her own home at the end of their meetings so the children would not be alone during the night. He helped her with small amounts of money so that she could pay her bills.

Now she asked her brothers to pay rent. In short order, Pauly, who had gotten a job on the waterfront, married a neighborhood girl and moved out. Lou became Luigi again and returned to Italy. Only Tony, the oldest of the three and a bit slower than the others, remained. He moved into the upstairs apartment and shared a room with his nephew, Steve. Josefina rented the downstairs apartment and appreciated the money that it brought in. Tony became the de facto janitor, keeping the halls clean, sweeping the outside street, making repairs. On nice summer days he went to the neighborhood playground and played bocci with the old men who congregated there and nights he watched television.

To cover the time she spent away from home with Von Holsten she told everyone she had an evening job as a waitress, something that sounded plausible and acceptable, so that she could be away for a few hours every night without causing suspicion or embarrassment.

Chapter 63

Unanswered Questions

The only one who still had questions was Detective Harley. He knew the Captain had rushed the case to closure and wondered why, since Von Holsten was usually as determined as a bulldog about tracking down such tenuous evidence. He thought about asking, but decided to bide his time.

Chapter 64

At the Whiteman's

At the Whiteman home, the family, devastated by Gigi's death, now had two small children to take care of. They never knew what became of the house in Spring Valley, nor did they care to know. The baby girl was only a few months old, little Larry was nearly five.

Among the friends who came to pay a shiva (condolence) call on the grieving Whiteman family was an old friend, Mrs. Levitz. She was a woman from the old country who had done well in the USA, her new country. Among her friends Mrs. Levitz was called an "all-rightnik," a person who had prospered since coming to America. She knew many people and had arranged several marriages and other alliances. When she saw the pretty baby that the sisters were passing from hand to hand she kept the picture in her mind. A few weeks after the shiva period, long after the seven days of mourning were over, she came to Mrs. Whiteman with a suggestion.

"It's very hard to start all over again with a baby, no Malka?" she asked. Mrs. Whiteman, depressed and exhausted, nodded yes. The woman said she knew people desperate for a baby, and that they would compensate the Whitemans' handsomely if they could adopt the little girl. The child would have a normal family life with people who would adore her. She spoke of all the reasons this would be a good idea. Mrs. Whiteman said she would let her know.

That night, she spoke to her husband and her daughters. All the girls were busy with their own lives, so they did not reject the suggestion. Reuben Whiteman could not look at the innocent babe without being reminded that she represented the death and destruction of his beautiful daughter. They all agreed it would be a mitzvah, a blessing, to give this child to people who were desperate for a child to love. Only Larry wondered about what was happening to his baby sister and if they were going to give him away too. They assured him they would never do that.

Chapter 65

Larry

In time the household settled into a routine. Larry started school and turned out to be a bright, pleasant child. His teachers knew nothing of his background or why he lived with his grandparents. Many grandmothers were raising grandchildren. One of the Whiteman daughters was not yet married and still lived at home. She often took care of Larry and played with him in the evening until his bedtime.

That lasted until she too began going steady and no longer had time for Larry. He missed his playtime with her. Mrs. Whiteman filled in as best she could but the little boy spent a lot of time alone. He had a room of his own and a few toys but hardly anyone to play with. Mr. Whiteman was feeling his age. When he came home from work he had dinner, then sat down with the day's paper and promptly fell asleep. He'd awaken in time to see the child being put to bed. As Larry grew older and made friends at school he was discouraged from bringing his classmates home. The tired, aging Whiteman's couldn't stand the noise of boisterous children. Larry Stark grew into a teenager who was often very lonely. They never heard from his father who now lived in Los Angeles with his new family.

Chapter 66

At the Fiorelli's

Josefina watched her children grow into teenagers. Unlike herself, they were being raised in a one-parent home, but they had had uncles who lived right downstairs, close enough to take on the male role model. And then Uncle Tony moved in with them. When they were a bit older and began asking questions about their father, about his death and what had happened those years before, Josefina told them there had been a terrible accident, a gas leak, which caused his death. They asked who his "friend" was and she told them just a family friend who had come to visit. Yet, each time she told them about the "terrible accident," she became more troubled. She had hoped the children, and in fact everyone in her world, would forget about that day. However, memory, her own and that of others, persisted and she began to sense that the story had not yet ended.

She continued to date Captain Von Holsten secretly. For a year their relationship was one of great passion. They indulged each other's every pleasure in the privacy of his home. He had a summer bungalow at Rockaway Beach, in an area that was virtually deserted in the winter. In time, familiarity made them a bit blasé, and the excitement began to wane. Yet neither wanted to end the relationship, and not just because of the lovemaking. They remembered the long days of loneliness before they came together and Josefina was nagged by a feeling of having forgotten something.

Josefina felt an edge of discomfort growing in her mind and though she could not pinpoint the cause, she found herself drawn to church. She had never been especially religious, often mocking the ladies in black who went faithfully each morning. One day she joined that procession, though still wearing her housedress and cardigan, and found a sense of peace in the cool, stony quiet of the neighborhood house of worship. She went early in the day when the children left for school, not wanting to meet anyone she knew. She never approached the confessional. She went regularly until she decided to take the children one Sunday morning. They were appropriately dressed and sat among the congregation. That day the priest gave a sermon in words that struck at her heart.

He said" God knows what you are inside, not the face that you show to the world. God knows what you have done wrong and what you have done right, even when no one else in the world knows. He is weighing and measuring you for the world to come…" and he continued in this vein until the end of the sermon. She imagined the words were aimed directly at her, that someone or something knew of her sins. Josefina lost her appetite for the church and no longer went in the mornings.

The children had been told their father had died in a freak accident and while they asked few questions, they seemed satisfied with the fairly noncommittal answers. He had, after all, been only an occasional visitor in the house as they were growing up. By the time they were old enough to think more about the incident, they were busy with their own lives and wanted to know less.

Chapter 67

Josefina's Affair

On rare occasions Captain Von Holsten came to her home and the children met him. One day Von Holsten asked her son Steve, now a teenager, if he'd like to go to a ball game with him, but both were uncomfortable in each other's presence. Maria, who hardly ever looked directly at him, thought he was huge, florid and forbidding, unlike her uncles who were familiar, short and dark. Both children wondered what he was doing in their home. Josefina understood their reluctance and did not press them to like Von Holsten. In any case, she wanted him in a separate and private part of her life and was not pleased when he came to the house but could think of no way to tell him to stay away.

The years went by so quickly, each seemed to step on the heels of the one in front. Josefina, like all mothers, saw her babies suddenly turn into young adults. She complained that her daughter wore too much makeup, wore her hair "too big" and her clothes too tight. Her son disappeared for long hours with friends she did not know. While she continued the fiction of a night job, Von Holsten became less generous than he had been and although money was tight, she was too proud to ask for more.

The children, however, needed and demanded more as they grew older. Since they were now in school throughout the day and had many activities after school, she decided she would actually try to find a real job. Noticing a help wanted sign in a nearby diner window, she applied. She was hired as a cashier. By the time she came home, prepared dinner and tended to household chores, she was exhausted.

Chapter 68

Nightmares

Josefina began to find her sleep troubled. She began having strange dreams of violence and death that awakened her in a sweat. She found that seeing Von Holsten was becoming a chore too, and she could find fewer reasons to explain going out nights now that she worked days. She had a harder time making excuses to Von Holsten to explain why she wouldn't see him.

Von Holsten, however, still desired the warmth he found in her body. Their sex was less hectic but more comfortable for him. One day he came to the restaurant where she worked and took her out during her lunch hour. He had found a hotel nearby and they spent the hour in bed. Strangely, she found this titillating and the excitement of their relationship sparked for a while. They began to meet at odd times, she making excuses to the children for not being able to come home right after work or telling them she was going out with friends on weekends. They wondered who these friends were, since they never met anyone that might qualify, but they never asked. Before long, the children had dates of their own and didn't care if she was there or not when they came home. She knew she should keep a better watch on what they did and whom they saw, but she was caught up in her own reinvigorated affair.

Chapter 69

Josefina's Children

Stephano, whom everyone called Steve, had grown into a handsome young fellow. At 18, he had the best features of both parents, his father's blue eyes, his mother's golden brown hair. He was well-built but his easy life had not given him the power and strength of his father. Maria, her daughter, had both her father's black hair and blue eyes, and by the time she was 16, she had developed her mother's voluptuous body. The children were bright, did well in school and were popular. Josefina swelled with pride at the sight of them but felt a nagging fear that she was not giving enough time to them, that she should know more of what they were doing with their time. To herself she rationalized the lack of attention by saying that the brother now living with her provided some sort of familial oversight. Even the brother who had married a neighborhood woman and lived nearby still provided a family tie.

Chapter 70

The Aha! Answer

A short time after the original Fiorelli case had been declared closed, Detective Harley was transferred out of the precinct to a station in the Bronx. He knew it was because he had continued to question the captain's decision in the case. Some months after his transfer it was by coincidence that he bumped into Von Holsten and Josefina at Sardi's, when Harley and his wife went there after a show. At once he understood the reason "the case was closed." He nodded to them and walked on, accepting the reality that life goes on – for some, especially after death.

Chapter 71

Changes, Once Again

But things were changing in the relationship, especially for Josefina. She was feeling tired and again pressured by Von Holsten. Familiarity was breeding in him, if not contempt, then a feeling of entitlement. He began to demand more of her time, and he proposed gratifications she was not prepared to deliver -- performances that made her feel debased as his own sexual powers waned. When she suggested that it might be wise to end their relationship he hinted that he might reopen her husband's death investigation. Over the years she had not quite succeeded in putting "the incident" out of her thoughts. With Von Holsten's innuendoes she was beginning to feel trapped like a fish in a net. Then, as she started having fearsome dreams again, Josefina needed somewhere to turn to find peace. More than ever, she looked to her children for satisfaction, for a sense that she had achieved something good in her life.

Chapter 72

Next Generations

Malka Whiteman never fully recovered from Gigi's death. She lost the tireless energy and ready laugh that had drawn people to her. Raising her grandson lay heavily on her peace of mind. She knew she could not give Larry the attention he so craved, to take him to interesting and educational places, or just go to a movie or a show with him. She just didn't have the strength for a young boy. Both she and her husband were aging too quickly. Yet, in spite of a sense that something wasn't right with his life, Larry Whiteman was growing up to be a good person, a mensch. Malka hoped he would meet a "nice Jewish girl" in the future and think of settling down.

Also much on her mind were the occasional reports she'd get from her friend Mrs. Levitz, about the baby girl who had been given for adoption. Even though the child's new life was supposed to be confidential and off limits to the Whiteman family, Mrs. Levitz knew it eased her friend Malka to know the little girl was much loved, healthy and doing well.

One afternoon Larry, now a teenager, asked his grandmother questions about his father. She told him as much as she knew, that he lived in California, had remarried and had a new family. This she had learned from Gary's mother, Larry's other grandmother, who occasionally called. Larry called his other grandmother and got his father's phone number. When he called his father, he asked if he could come to California to meet with his Dad's new family, his half-sister and half-brother. After some hesitation, Gary, who was now doing well both financially and professionally, agreed, and said he would send a ticket.

When Larry and Gary met, they met as strangers. Gary didn't even recognize his son. That feeling remained the entire time Larry was in his father's home. Gary's second wife was only five years older than Larry and his step -sister and -brother were little kids. He felt no connection to this family nor did he feel any kinship with his father. After the visit, he felt more alone than ever. The baby sister who had disappeared from his life was for the most part, forgotten.

Larry was a good student and a talented artist. In his senior year at high school he tried for and won an art scholarship to Pratt University in Brooklyn. In college he began to hang out with friends who were as bright as he but who, like him, had too much time on their hands. They met at a local coffee shop and talked radical politics, about how they might save the world from the political hacks who were running and ruining it.

Sometimes they would meet in each other's homes where there was seldom a parent present. They experimented with marijuana and alcohol – and sex. Larry was hungry for affection and for a connection, someone to call his own. He latched on to a pretty girl in the group, Amaranth, whose own busy family left her with similar needs and ideas and a lot of free time. But as graduation neared, all the kids in the group started to drift off into other directions, other pastimes and finally out of each others lives.

Malka and Reuven Whiteman stood alongside Larry with great pride as graduation pictures were snapped. They knew he had been through tough times and appreciated that he had come this far with the little support they could offer, both spiritually and financially. His college friends, both the young women and the men, gathered round to shake his hand, kiss his cheek, hug and wish well to each other. Under their gowns they wore shorts and sneakers and sandals. There was a bittersweet feel in the atmosphere as this phase of their lives was ending.

Chapter 73

What's Next

On the way home Larry and his grandparents had little to say to one another, each lost in his or her own thoughts. Malka thought of what the boy had been through since early childhood. Although much loved, he had been raised by elderly grandparents who were out of touch with his world. His aunts and cousins were involved in their own lives and families and had little time to include him. Holidays were celebrated together but not much else. He hardly remembered his mother and by now only knew her from photos in an album. He never heard from his distant father or those in his father's family. Larry wondered what the next days would bring now that he was no longer a student, no longer had a place to go each weekday morning. His part-time job in a hardware store could not be his future. Before leaving Pratt he had met with counselors and had a few leads for jobs in art work but even then he did not know the direction he wished to travel.

"Grandma, on Monday I'll have to 'hit the bricks' as they say and start looking for a job", Larry reminded. "Wake me up at six in the morning, okay?" She nodded yes, noting the concern in his eyes. And with that in mind, they went home. All his aunts, uncles and cousins and a few neighbors had gathered in the house and prepared a surprise celebratory lunch. The mood was festive and loving and his anxiety faded.

Larry's skill and talent were obvious and he landed a job in short order with a comic book studio. It was a job he loved. As a kid he had grown up with the company of comic books. He even created his own super hero – a lonely kid who could blink whatever he wanted into reality. Now, although just doing fill-in work for the senior artists at the company, he envisioned a time when he would be a full-fledged artist doing his own strip. He made many friends at the studio and began going out with them. After a short time his salary and self-confidence had increased enough for him to consider moving from his grandparent's house and getting an apartment of his own.

Chapter 74

One of the women he worked with at the studio was a firebrand type who took on causes. Her name was Eva Emmer. She was five or six years older than Larry and he admired her spirit. Her latest crusade was to have one of the old warehouses under the Manhattan Bridge refurbished and rented out to what she deemed "starving artists" for below market rates. She'd been haranguing an elderly landlord who owned a building that was in danger of becoming a wreck. He repeatedly told her that the property was zoned for "commercial only." She pointed out that if he rented only to artists the property would be considered workspaces and would qualify as commercial.

Since the building had been empty for years he gave it consideration. Some income would be better than none, he thought. He wondered how much he would have to invest to make it worth his while. It would involve some serious fumigation for the many kinds of animal life now comprising the only tenancy. Structurally the five floors of the property were solid, but the interior had become a mess of debris, untouched by broom, water or paint for several years. After much negotiation, he agreed to a deal that would have him do basic cleanup and repair but all décor would be the responsibility of the tenants.

Larry joined the list of people interested in renting space. They could put two studios on each floor and there was a rudimentary toilet on each floor, so renters would have to install a bathroom, one from scratch, in each apartment. Basic kitchens had to be installed as well. Nevertheless, every space was snatched up by friends who were invited to join the project. There were many from the comic book company where Larry worked, a few musicians, dancers, actors and in what seemed only moments, the space was fully spoken for. The future tenants used savings and money borrowed from banks and family for the renovations. Much of the work was do-it-yourself by the mostly young people and before long the halls were clean and painted, bright lights installed, apartments took shape. The outside of the building gave no clue to what had been performed inside. Even though everyone had worked on it, the tenants felt it was a miracle.

Chapter 75

The New Home

Larry worked alongside Eva every free moment they could as they fixed the apartments on the floor they shared. They became friends. He admired her strength and determination, her artistic inventiveness and found that he liked the way she looked. Eva, a runner, was lean and tanned. She wore her hair short and it curled naturally, forming a frame around her face. He enjoyed her company and now that work on the apartments was completed, they could relax. They made dinner for one another or just sat with a beer in hand in one apartment or the other and talked. They invited company some nights and some evenings they played board games or watched TV. One such evening she sat near enough for him to put his arm around her. He pulled her closer to him and realized he didn't feel like a buddy or pal. He was reacting to her closeness, the clean smell of her soap, the warmth emanating from her skin. He turned her face to his, looked into her eyes and kissed her mouth. She returned his kiss with a feeling that surprised him. When he felt her tongue in his mouth his body formed its own response. They had connected. Here was another beginning.

Chapter 76

The Baby Sister

As Larry grew older he seemed to forget that there had ever been a sister. He knew nothing of her life, just that she had been adopted. Although Malka knew, he did not know that the baby girl had been adopted by a Navy lawyer by the name of Andrew Walton and his wife, Helene. They had named the baby Ronni. She was dearly loved and doted upon and was never in want for anything – emotionally or physically . She had a warm and pleasant personality and many good friends. As she reached her teens she was an outstanding student and growing more beautiful each day as the braces and awkwardness of the pre-teen years disappeared. She had Gigi's heart-shaped face and huge dark eyes and Gerry's long spidery eyelashes. By the time she entered high school her figure had developed the same dancer's lines as her birth mother's. Her parents glowed at the sight of her.

Chapter 77

Baby Grows Up

She'd been less than a year old when Helene and Andrew took her. She had never learned that she was adopted. She knew only this beloved Mom and Dad as her true family. There were no shadows -- no memory of a brother, grandparents or aunts, nor of any other mother or father.

In time, her Dad retired from the Navy and moved back to New York City and got a job at a "white shoe" law firm. She started high school in the city, having passed the test for Stuyvesant, one of the city's most selective high schools. In her freshman year she met a young man in the school's art class they both took. She liked him and they became friends after he worked with her on a class project. He was a senior, good-looking and smart and fun to be around. His name was Steve Fiorelli. They shared an interest in art and were drawn to one another. They "hung out" together and in time, began to date.

After graduation from high school, Steve applied to various city colleges. His mother was a single parent and could not afford an expensive private college but his artistic talent helped him get into Cooper Union with a substantial scholarship. He found part-time work to cover some of the expenses. Two years later, the youngsters were still seeing each other. When Ronni graduated from high school three years later, her parents could afford to send her to a private out-of-town college. With a 3.9 average she could have a choice of schools but decided to go to New York University in order to be near both the comfort of her home -- and Steve. By then he worked as an intern at an architecture firm in the city. They saw each other at every opportunity. Ronni and Steve dated throughout the years she was in college. Josefina was aware that he was seeing the same someone since high school but was not particularly curious about whom she might be. She thought of it as puppy love, forgetting she had been married for a few years at his age.

Around their friends, Ronni and Steve were "an item." But Ronni wasn't happy about some of the hippie friends that Steve hung out with. She never wanted to go where they went or do the things they did. She exerted a strong influence on him and was beginning to draw him away from them. Then again, Steve was not too pleased with the friends Ronni surrounded herself, finding they lacked seriousness, were uninvolved with the world around them and rather lightweight in their lifestyles. But he and she were so deeply into one another that each gave up some of the outside world to be together in their private one.

Chapter 78

Meeting the Parents

Ronni talked about Steve to her mom and dad. Of course his name had no special meaning for them. The name on their baby's birth certificate and adoption papers had read Jerrilyn Whiteman and they named her Ronni. When Steve Fiorelli came to the Walton's home to pick Ronni up her parents found him personable and intelligent. They didn't anticipate where the relationship might lead, but it was comforting to know their daughter had a boyfriend who seemed a decent, dependable young man.

After the years of steady dating, Steve brought Ronni home to meet his mother. Something about the young woman troubled Josefina. She was pretty enough but Josefina was most concerned that she wasn't Catholic. Also, she had an air of confidence about herself that Josefina found arrogant, forgetting her own youthful attitude to her parents. She reminded her of someone, but try as she would to think of whom, she could not pin down an identification. Josefina suggested to Steve that he might want to try dating some other girls and not yet tie himself down to one person.

Steve looked at his mother questioningly. "Why do you say that, Mom. Ronni is wonderful and the only one I want to be with. I love her and she loves me."

Josefina didn't know why she felt strange about the girl, just that she did. "Well, you know son, she isn't Catholic. That could make life complicated, don't you think?" she countered.

"Ma, how Catholic are we? You hardly ever go to church anymore and I never go," he responded. "Anyway, even though we want to be together, we have a long way to go before we think of getting married. She has to finish college, I'm trying to grow in my job and Ronni will probably want to work for a while too. So don't worry about it, okay."

Chapter 79

Why Worry

The nagging feeling, however, wouldn't let go. She spoke to Von Holsten about it but couldn't make sense of her unease to him either. A few weeks later, Von Holsten, who didn't have enough to do with his time since retiring from the police force, decided to nose around a bit. He knew Steve spent a lot of his free time on the campus of NYU where his girlfriend was a student. He spotted him at the school, walking with his arm around a girl. He tried as unobtrusively as possible to get closer to get a better look at the young woman. From a short distance away he admired the shapely figure, the proud posture. When he came closer he looked at the beautiful girl and felt a shock of recognition at the sight of her. As a trained policeman, he caught the resemblance immediately. If her long hair were darker and parted in the middle she was a ringer for the unfortunate girl that had died in Josefina's apartment some 20 years ago! No wonder Josefina felt there was something familiar about her. How could she have missed it?

Before jumping to any conclusion, he decided to investigate. He began an inquiry into the young woman's background. It took weeks of requisitions and showing his badge before he got some answers. He learned that Ronni's father was an attorney, her mother a stay-at-home housewife, an active volunteer in many charities and non-profits. They became parents, as expected, some twenty years before, but they were adoptive parents. When he traced further, he confirmed what he suspected. The girl was the daughter of the dead woman and Steve's own father, Gerry Fiorelli, and she was Steve Fiorelli's half sister!

Von Holsten was at a loss about what to do. He wasn't even sure he should tell Josefina what he had learned. The youngsters were, obviously, deeply in love. Dozens of questions raced through his thoughts. How to tell Steve that Ronni was his half-sister; how to explain the events of his father's death and how it had happened, as well as its aftermath. How to explain Von Holsten's own part in all this? Steve was a smart young man. How long would it be before there were probing questions about his father's death? About his mother's part in it? Von Holslten never doubted that Josefina and her brothers had murdered the couple. He'd wondered, over the years, what Josefina had told her children about their father's death, about the two bodies found in their kitchen. Having been instrumental in making the case disappear, he never wanted to know and had never asked. Now what, he wondered.

Chapter 80

Revelations

The next time he and Josefina were together he was unusually quiet. She noticed and asked if anything was wrong.

"Well, yes, there is something on my mind. It's something to do with Steve, and I don't know how to tell you," he trailed off. Josefina paled.

"Tell me. What's happened to my son," she whispered.

"He's fine, nothing happened to him. It's…well, it's just that the girl he is seeing, Ronni Walton…and well, you were right there is something about her."

"I knew it, I knew it. She's a bum, right, a puta, and she has him altogether fooled," Josefina said triumphantly.

"No," said Von Holsten, "that's not it. It's hard to tell you this, Jo. You said there was something about her that bothered you, right? Didn't she remind you of someone?"

Josefina thought for a minute and began to wonder what he was leading up to. Suddenly, she went white, then her face flushed red. She looked into Von Holsten's eyes.

"No, no, canna be," she said, her accent coming on strong. "Who this devil?"

"C'mon Jo, the girl's no devil. She's the daughter of your husband and the woman who died on your kitchen floor," he blurted out. "The kid was adopted by a nice family but she's your son's half-sister. And that's the girl he's in love with."

Josefina held her head in her hands. In the years since the "incident," she had never acknowledged the horrible dreams and had maintained denial even to herself but deep inside herself she had waited for retribution. She had heard the phrase, "waiting for the other shoe to drop" and now she understood what it meant. She wondered what the punishment would be, knowing that this was not the end of the matter but another beginning.

"What should we do," she asked, the misery pouring from her eyes. Von Holsten heard the "we."

"I don't know what to say, how to advise you," he answered. "It could open a Pandora's Box." Josefina had no idea what that meant but understood it was not a good thing.

They both remained mute, staring at one another.

Chapter 81

Confessions

A few evenings later, both Josefina's children came home to dinner, something that was happening less and less. As she cooked, as she set the table and put condiments in the center, she kept sighing, sighs that seemed to come up from her shoes. As Steve and Maria told her how they'd spent their day, she answered absentmindedly, "Yeah, nice. Oh good," and other noncommittal responses that made it clear to the youths that she had not heard a word they had said, as she blew another deep sigh.

"Ma, what's the matter?" asked Steve.

"Are you sick, Mama?" Maria questioned, a concerned look on her face.

Josefina turned to look at her children. "You know my life has not been easy," she said in Italian. They were surprised, then, at her speaking in the language she seldom used since they had grown up -- and were now sure something was wrong. They became apprehensive and looked at their mother expectantly. She could no longer hold back her "secret" and in a monotone that sounded like an Italian funeral dirge, she explained.

"You know that when you were little your father and I were not getting along – had not been for a long time. Well, you might as well know that he was having an affair. You were too young to understand that when he died." Another deep sigh. "But what none of us knew was that he had a child with that woman. I just found out that you have a – a

-- a half-sister." She had difficulty saying the words. While tears started to run down Josefina's cheeks her two children sat stunned, silent.

Steve asked, "Does that have something to do with the way Dad and that woman died?"

Josefina looked up at him and nodded, yes. "They committed suicide."

"Here," Steve asked, incredulous. Maria sat shaking her head in bewilderment. "I don't understand any of this Mama. What's happening to us? Why didn't we know anything about all this before."

"You were too young when it happened. When you got older, you never asked so I said nothing," moaned Josefina. The kitchen grew silent again, except for Josefina's sighs and an occasional sob. She dreaded what was to come.

"There's more to this, isn't there Ma," asked Steve. Maria looked sharply at her brother.

"What else could there be? Mama, are we able to meet this girl? Where does she live? Does she know about us? What else do you know about her?" Maria queried.

Josefina sat down heavily on a kitchen chair. She began to sob, deep, wrenching sobs. The other shoe was about to drop. Steve, feeling deeply his mother's distress, got up and kneeled in front of her, caressing her arm.

"Mama, it will be all right. Nothing could be so bad. You have us. Finish telling us and we'll know what to do," he said.

When she took her hands away from her face, they were shocked to see she looked years older, her face fallen and lined, wet with her tears.

"You already met her," she whispered to her son. "She is Ronni, the girl you brought to meet me."

Stephano fell back on his rear end, stunned, his face reflecting his shock, as though he had been punched. Maria jumped up and stared first at her mother then her brother. No one spoke. Then everyone spoke.

Maria said, "What are you talking about, how do you know that?" Steve said, bitterly, "You're just saying that because you don't want me to see her anymore!" Josefina said, "I wish that was the case," and began crying once more.

Steve, after thinking a bit, asked, "Does Von Holsten know this? I saw him on campus at Ronni's school. Was he following me?"

Josefina lifted a tear-stained, pained face. Miserably, she nodded yes.

Ma, you met him when they investigated Dad's death, didn't you," he queried. "You know him a long time."

Josefina's voice turned cold, her face stony. "What you sayin," she asked in English.

Maria turned her attention to her brother. "What's going on, Steve?"

"Ma, did you kill Dad?"

Maria's eyes bugged out. "Steve, what are you talking about?"

Chapter 82

Anguish

Josefina's eyes closed as the memory of that day flooded back upon her. She began to speak Italian, again in a bleak monotone. Her voice seemed to come from a distance.

"You would not understand. I came from a world where we got even. La vendetta. They had cheated me of a husband and my children of their father. I could not let that stand. I did what I had to, to keep my honor."

Her daughter's face drained of color. Steve sat down on a chair, heavily, his elbows on his knees, his head in his hands. She looked at him and thought of Gerry, seeing the father in the gestures of the son.

When Steve looked up at his mother, he was looking at a stranger, or more than that, at an enemy. Josefina saw the hate and wrath in his eyes.

"No, you, you took my father from me. And then you became Von Holsten's whore so he would keep your secret. Tell me, how many lives will you have destroyed for your '*honor*?'" His voice was venomous, the loathing in his eyes like beams, scorching his mother. How do I tell Ronni that my mother killed her mother? What happens now to my love, my life?" He stood up and stalked from the apartment.

Josefina's daughter looked lost. Maria stood and cried. "Mama, what did you do? Her world too, was caving in on her. Her mother was her rock and now it was crumbling. What are we supposed to do now," she asked. "No, no, don't me tell anything, you can't give me any advice. You're evil."

"Maria, I'm still your mother. I love you and want to do what's right for all of us," she reverted to speaking Italian. We will go on with our lives as before."

"Nothing can go on as before, Mama. Can Steve go on with his life? He loves Ronni but he can never marry her, no matter what, no matter how this turns out. She's his sister. No, your advice is not good," said Maria, tears streaming down her cheeks. The cocoon that was her world had shattered. Her mother reached for her to hold her close, but Maria pulled back, turned to the door and ran from the house.

Josefina stood in the kitchen that had been home base for more than twenty-five years, more alone than ever in her life. She had no way of knowing what the next days held for her. This, she thought, is the punishment I have been expecting. What would her beloved Stephano do, she agonized. And Von Holsten. Would he turn her in to the police. No, he could not because he was just as guilty as she. Her world too, was crumbling around her, the walls seemed to close in, compressing even the air she breathed. She was right to worry.

Chapter 83

A Grandmother's Second Sorrow

Steve wandered the familiar streets around his home, not knowing where he was going, finding nothing familiar in the neighborhood where he had spent his life. Like an automaton, he walked into the subway and got off the train at his grandmother's station.. He climbed her steps as though he had lead weights on his ankles and knocked on her door. Just one look at his face made her pull him into the house.

"What happen," she asked.

He sat on a kitchen chair and, echoing his mother's dirge-like monotone, poured out the story that had just unfolded, leaning forward, his hands hanging limply between his knees.

"Grandma, I think I want to die. I can never be with the woman I love. She's my sister."

Once again Concetta's heart felt the shriveling she'd known so many years before as she watched another beautiful young man run down a country road, away from her and her love. She stood behind his chair and put her arms around his neck, cradling his head on her chest.

"Oh, I know this gonna have a bitter end. It's my fault too, 'cause I send you faddah back to Italy for a wife. Dat place not lucky for him. My poor boy, this too hard for me to live wit. I shoulda been buried before my son but God din't call me. What I will tell you now, you gotta keep on livin'. Life finds a way to wash out dese hurts. You'll see.

"Grandma, can I stay here? I can't go back to that house, to my mother, the murderer."

"Stephano, caro mia, you could stay here long as you want. But a

Lillian Lee Liss

mother is a mother. If you kill somebody, she would never turn herself away from you. She suffering too. Don't turn away from her. Maybe she need you more now. You gotta try to unnerstan. Where she come from, they believe in that garbage, la vendetta. That were my son, my child, she kill. She tink she get away wit it, but I know what she did. But what's done is done and nobody could change what happen. Dead is dead. But you, you young and 'live and you gotta make the best. You heart, she break, I know about that, but we could live wit broken hearts.

Chapter 84

Seeking Truth

Life tugged at him. He sifted through a thousand ways to meet and speak with Ronni, to tell her of this tragedy. Then he thought he had better speak with her parents first, to find out if there was truth in her being adopted and if he and she shared a father.

Steve Fiorelli called the Walton's home and asked to speak with them, making a formal-sounding appointment. Thinking he wanted to discuss marriage, they met him at the door with smiles. He didn't know how to begin and looked grim, almost ill. They realized something was wrong, that perhaps their daughter had had an accident or that he was ending his relationship with Ronni and became apprehensive. They didn't want her hurt in any way.

"What did you want to see us about, Steve," questioned Andrew Walton, the smile gone from his face.

Steve didn't know how to begin. He looked around at the warm living room, lined with books, paintings and souvenirs from their travels. He sat down without being invited.

"I have to ask you some questions that you might find strange. At least I hope you find them strange," he began. He looked at Helene Walton and blurted, "Is Ronni adopted?"

Helene moved back as though struck, a startled look on her face. "That is a strange question for you to ask. Why do you want to know. What has that to do with you?" she said in a somewhat offended tone.

The misery that swept over Steve's face made her regret her tone immediately. "Steve, what is it. What's going on. Is Ronni all right?"

In a voice choking with emotion he replied, "Ronni's fine. She doesn't know I'm here or why. But once I know the answer to what I'm asking that might change. Is she an adopted child?"

Helene and Andrew Walton exchanged meaningful looks. Andrew said, "Yes, she is, but Ronni doesn't know. We saw no reason to tell her and she came to us when she was just a few months old. She never knew any other parents but us. You must tell us what is going on. It sounds like something terrible is happening."

Before he could speak, Steve dropped his head into his hands and started to sob. "Oh my God, it's true, it's true, came out with his muffled sobs.

Helene got up and sat beside him. She put her arm around his shoulders.

"Tell us, Steve," she said.

He pulled himself together and dried his face on his handkerchief and began an explanation in a voice that had the sound of a death knell. He looked directly at the Waltons.

"Today I found out that before my father died he had an affair. He and this woman, who also died, had a child, a girl. When she was just a few months old, the baby was adopted by people who became her loving parents.

Looking at the Waltons he could see the blood drain from Helene's face while Andrew's flushed red. He knew they had already reached a conclusion before he said any more.

"Oh my God," said Helene Walton, in a whisper. "You're sister and brother. My poor baby. You poor boy." Tears ran down her cheeks without a sound.

Andrew could say nothing, he could hardly breathe. He thought of his happy daughter and what this would do to her. He looked at the young man, seeing clearly the misery he felt. His own misery already matched Steve's.

Chapter 85

Painful Truths

"Who will tell Ronni," Helene asked. As they stared at each other, a voice came from the doorway.

"Tell Ronni what?" said Ronni. Then, looking at the devastated faces, she lost her smile and asked what had happened.

"What are you doing here, Steve?" Three grown people sat speechless, staring at a young woman each of them loved, deeply, completely

"Sit down, Ron," said Steve. "We need to talk."

"Did someone die?" Ronni wanted to know. How do I answer that, thought Steve, since as far as he was concerned, the answer was yes, I'm dying as you watch. He began to recite what was now fact.

As the story spun out the young woman's beautiful face seemed to sink in on itself. As her eyes opened wider the cheeks pulled in, the mouth became a grim line.

"This is ridiculous. Stop talking. I don't believe any of this," Ronni almost shouted, anguish in her voice. Once again Steve dropped his head into his hands. He could not look at her, and though he wanted to take her in his arms and comfort her, he could not reach out to touch her. He could almost feel a bar between them, physically separating the lovers.

"Mom, Dad," she implored, "tell me what this is all about. I can't understand what's happening here. Are you telling me now, that you're not my real father and mother? Are you saying that Steve is my brother?

We are planning to get married when I graduate and we get jobs. What's happening to my life?" She began to cry, heart-wrenching sobs.

Helene Walton went to her daughter, held her and rocked her, much as she did during the bad days of her childhood.

"I'm so sorry, baby. We didn't think you would benefit by knowing you were adopted. We never dreamt it would come back to haunt us like this." She tried to soothe the young woman who was her world, her love.

The stricken parents suggested to Steve that he leave so they could talk over what had happened. He went to the door, his steps dragging as though he had aged fifty years.

Chapter 86

Misery

Steve went to his grandmother's house. He couldn't bring himself to return to his mother's home. How could he ever face her again, he wondered, even though what his grandmother had said stayed in his mind. He saw Ronni's tightened face, heard her near hysteria as she refused to listen to any more and this reinforced the new hatred he felt for his mother.

Then he was torn by his long-standing love and new-found pity for Josefina. She had stood behind him in all his endeavors, had cared for him with devotion all the years of his life. She had lived with a terrible secret for so many years, protecting her children from desertion with her body. His head spun with confusion and indecision. His grandmother knocked and came into the room with a drink in her hands.

"Drink this, my boy. It will help you sleep," she said as she offered him a hot cup of tea that smelled of vermouth and lemon. He wanted to sleep and not think any more, so he took the cup and sipped. She sat down next to him on the bed and just leaned against him until he put his arm around her small shoulders.

The drink and the comfort made his eyes close and he lay down. His grandmother removed his shoes and pulled the blanket over him and he slept.

Chapter 87

Endings and Beginnings

Only Steve slept, the sleep of the drugged. His grandmother went to her room and cried the night away. Josefina sat in the same kitchen chair she had been in all evening, throughout the night. Maria came back to the house and told her mother she was moving in with her boyfriend, a young man Josefina hated for his uncouth demeanor and appearance. She knew that this was not the time to try to stop her and watched, mutely, miserably, as her daughter packed a suitcase.

Ronni locked herself in her room and spent the night looking out the window. She sat, dry-eyed, as she tried to organize her swirling thoughts, trying to think of what might come next. Helene and Andrew Walton sat on the sofa half the night, holding hands. They wondered if they would ever again be able to provide joy to their beloved daughter, now that she knew the truth of her birth, while suffering the loss of her lover.

When Steve woke up all that happened rushed back into his mind. Finally, he could think about the situation without the emotional trauma of yesterday's revelations. He needed to speak with Ronni. He dressed and went to the kitchen to have breakfast with his grandmother. Concetta eyed her grandson warily. He was too calm to suit her.

"How you feel today, Stephano," she asked. He looked long and hard at his grandmother.

"I have to find a way to make this right," he answered. "I'm thinking. I don't have the answer yet but I will. You know, Grandma, we are all victims of what my mother did. Maybe she thought she was entitled to do what she did but she was wrong. Why should Ronni and I have to pay the price for my father's and her mistakes?" He continued to talk, mostly mumbling to himself.

Concetta listened to what sounded to her like rambling and wondered if she could do anything to help. She had run out of suggestions and advice.

Steve called the Walton house and asked to speak with Ronni. She got on the phone with a listless "Hi." He asked her to meet him on campus. Ronni was glad to get out of the house but didn't know what to expect when she met Steve.

Chapter 88

Solutions

When they met, he took her in his arms and held her. She clung to him as though to a lifeline. They spoke for an hour then each went their separate ways. For two weeks both were so busy, the adults in their lives saw little of them. Helene and Andrew were relieved that Ronni had gone back to school and to her regular routine but were concerned that she did not mention what had happened.

Concetta watched as Steve spent every waking hour on the computer he had brought from home. He wrote letters that he immediately took to the corner mailbox. He seemed deeply preoccupied with a project. She didn't know what was going on but was pleased that he was busy and no longer despairing.

Then, they both disappeared. When Ronni didn't come home from school her parents were not concerned until the sky darkened and they had not heard from her. Concetta thought Steve may have gone home to Josefina's house. The telephone calls didn't start until after midnight. The next day they called the police, fearing the worst.

Upon examination, they found that clothing and whatever was of value to the pair had disappeared as well. They were dumbfounded at the thought they had run away together, leaving no word or clue.

A search of was initiated of airlines, train stations and buses. The Waltons hired detectives to continue the search after the police stopped investigating. One year passed, then a second. Two more years ticked by. No one heard from Ronni or Steve and the police added whatever details they had to the cold case file. The families lived with pain and uncertainty until, little by little, they became inured to the loss.

Chapter 89

Some Answers

Six years after the disappearance, a large, manila envelope came to both Grandma Concetta and to the Waltons. In it was an 8X10 photo of Ronni and Steve each holding a small, red-haired, green-eyed child, all smiling broadly. There was no background, no return address and the postmark was so smudged no one could make it out. The Waltons let out what felt like a long-held breath. They studied the picture for clues but were happy at the obvious joy and contentment on all four faces.

Concetta had made a comfortable life for herself during the years in Brooklyn. Neighbors on all sides became friends. She invited them for her delicious home-cooked meals. When she told them she had been a seamstress in the old country, many brought garments for alterations, even to have clothes made. At first she refused to take any money from them but they left cash on the kitchen table. As people praised her fine work, a business grew in her kitchen and she earned a good living from the talent in her fingers. She was happy that she had work to keep her busy and no longer needed anyone's financial help.

Concetta called Josefina and told her about the photograph. For the first time in years, Josefina rushed to the home of her mother-in-law. She looked at the snapshot and burst into tears, and pressed it to her chest. Her sobs resonated in Concetta, who patted her shoulder. She looked at the old woman and asked, with a plea in her voice, "Can I have the picture? I'll make you a copy."

Concetta, showing the compassion learned over a life of strife, nodded assent. But with the great strength of her years, she spoke to her daughter-in-law in their familiar Italian and finally said what she had been feeling for so many years.

"You have done terrible things, woman, for your desperate pride. But the worst is what you have done to your children. You robbed them of both a father -- and a mother because now they know what you did and they hate you. Even though you are paying a bitter price, it is less than you deserve," the old woman said. "Now, go home. You never gave me the respect you should have and you will get from your children exactly what you gave to your elders," Concetta said to Josefina in the clear language of their home village.

Josefina paled at the old woman's words. When she turned to leave her step was that of an old woman, her head bent, her arms at her sides, her feet shushing along the floor. When she arrived home she called her daughter's house. An operator came on the line and said that the number she called had been changed and she gave a new number with an unfamiliar prefix. She called again with the new number. When she called, Maria answered the phone.

"Oh, Ma, I meant to call you to tell you we moved to New Jersey. Louie got a new job and we were so busy I just never got a chance to call. We only got here yesterday. Listen, I have to feed the baby. I'll get back to you as soon as I can, okay."

As though stabbed in her heart, Josefina just managed to say, "Grandma Concetta got a picture from Steve." Then she hung up, knowing that if for no other reason than those few words, she would hear from her daughter. The phone rang after a few minutes. She told Maria about the photograph.

"Make me a copy too. I'll give you my address so you can send it to me." There was no invitation to visit, no indication that she might come back to see her mother. Concetta's voice echoed in her head like a witch's curse. Whom could she speak with, to tell of her heartbreak? When she hung up the phone Josefina called Von Holsten, to tell him about the picture.

"No kidding. So that's what they did. That took nerve. Well, now you know they're okay." He made some small talk but gave no indication that he would be interested in seeing her. The apartment that had been a refuge for her suddenly felt like a prison cell, a solitary prison cell. There was no one else she could turn to for a kind word, for solace. She leaned over the table, her head resting on her arm and sat that way for a long time.

Chapter 90

Another New Start

People have been known to disappear from their homes and lifestyles with little explanation. New lives can begin – or – end without any seeming reason. Steve and Ronni had planned their new life carefully. They first had to decide to give up whatever life they had known before and leave those they dearly loved, without a clue. They moved to a busy southern city where people could come and go with no questions or curiosity. All the letters that Steve had sent out were job applications and rental inquiries. They decided on the city, went for interviews and applied for new forms of identification, much like the people in the federal witness program.

They found an apartment in a modern high rise building that seemed to promise anonymity. They created new backgrounds for previous lives. Jobs were found as their abilities were demonstrated and their new lives were launched. But the sadness of the existences they had shed, the loved ones they might never see again, haunted them. In time, the need for more than just each other became a reality. A young woman at Ronni's job became pregnant. She was on a fast track to promotion. After much discussion and planning, an agreement was reached for Ronni and Steve to adopt her child. It turned out she was pregnant with twins. That suited Ronni and Steve well. After the woman gave birth, Ronni left the job and opted to be a stay at home mom. Life was almost complete for the loving couple.

A few months later, another envelope arrived at the Walton's with another photo and a note that said, "We love you and miss you but you

Josefina's Honor

must understand that we have begun a new life and can never come back to New York. It would create too many complications. Perhaps one day we'll be together again, somehow, somewhere. We don't want to contact Steve's mother but please let Steve's grandmother know we are well and happy. She will be happy for us. If, one day you get a call and no one answers, it may be us, just so we can hear your voices and know all is well with you. Perhaps, when enough time has gone by, we'll speak again.

The Waltons hired another detective firm to try to trace the couple. After many dead ends, Andrew Walton said, "Let's stop looking. When they are ready they'll come to us or we will go to them. We know they are well and I'm sure they long to see us as much as we want to see them. We'll be together one day." In the detective's investigations he had learned of a loose end, the existence of another half-brother to Ronni. His name was Larry Whiteman.

Chapter 91

The Trail Goes On

Larry Whiteman had married Eva Emmer. They took down the wall between their two apartments. They now had two children and visited the elderly Whiteman's regularly, as well as all the aunts' families. That was when the Whiteman's contacted him and told him the whole tragic tale. In doing so, they gave Larry back his almost forgotten sister though at the moment, she was still lost as well as found. Still he felt he had found the closest missing part of his original family and this part of his life was no longer a mystery. So many things were coming together for him at last.

Chapter 92

A Puzzle Piece Fits In

Larry had found his own way in life. Aside from building his own family, his own happiness, he knew now that so many people loved him and shared his pleasures. He was an integral member of a large, extended family. He worked at a job he loved, made a good living and eventually bought a house of his own. He wanted another "starving artist" to have the opportunity to live in what he called "their lucky home."

Concetta passed away peacefully in her sleep. Her neighbors called Maria, not Josefina. They knew the young woman had her grandmother's burial plans. She took meticulous and loving care of all the funeral details. Josefina did not attend the funeral and missed seeing her daughter and her grandchildren. Maria sold the house her father had bought for his devoted mother so many years before, bought with such love and awe. The money was bequeathed to Maria to share with her brother. Concetta never stopped believing that someday Steve would return to the family.

Chapter 93

Josefina's Next Move

Josefina took stock of her world and decided there was no longer anything to hold her in Brooklyn, this place that she had come to so willingly and happily. It was supposed to be her refuge and comfort, her dream and her triumph. She put the house up for sale, and when it was sold, she gave all the furniture to the Salvation Army. Then she returned to Santa Teresa, to the home she'd so easily deserted many years before. When she arrived at the old tavern, she felt a sweep of her old arrogance run through her at the sight of the town, thinking, "I did it. I'm rich, I maintained my honor and should be admired."

She was a rich woman by the town's standards but no one noted or rejoiced at her return. She was a virtual stranger who had chosen a different path. Her parents were still alive, now very old. They barely recognized this middle-aged woman.

Many changes had been made to the old bar and the house . An addition had been built onto the back so the old people would not have to climb stairs and her brothers and their wives had taken over the business, which was now called Stephano's Ristorante. They kept the old-fashioned look of the dining room and the whole family worked there. It was a busy and popular place. Bus tours stopped there for the authenticity. The brothers had also grown rich.

When Josefina came back they let her use her old room. They knew she had her own money and they would not be responsible for her support. However, as was the custom, it was expected that as an unattached daughter she would tend to the needs of her mother and father until their demise. Her parents did not remember this woman as their beautiful young daughter and thought of her as a hired caregiver. She cleaned their soilings, bathed and dressed them, fed them and wiped their drooling chins. She too, did not know, did not recognize these two helpless, elderly relics. What had become of the powerful couple who were her mother and father, she wondered.

She was just 50 years old. Josefina felt there was no place in the world to which she belonged, no person to whom she was connected. It was then she put on the black dress, the black shoes and stockings and became a caricature of all she had hoped to escape when she left Santa Teresa. In a short time the once proud shoulders drooped under the black shawl, her walk became a shuffle. One evening, after a year had passed and she finished tending to her chores, she went into her small room, closed the door and lay down on her single bed. She felt that the lid on her coffin had just closed.

La Vendetta.

About the Author

She is Mother, Grandmother, Writer, Community Activist - in that order. Three grown sons and five grandkids are the most important facets of her busy life. She has served on the Boards of a hospital's mental health center, neighborhood housing organization, a community board, was president of a neighborhood association for 20 years, executive assistant to a local school board and an aide to the Deputy Chancellor of a major city school board. She wrote throughout all these years for local newspapers, house organs, wrote articles in local and religious presses (including the Village Voice of NY) and ghost wrote magazine articles for many employers. Now she writes the many stories collected in her head over the years.

Today she is a super-volunteer as a museum docent, cooks for an elderly and handicapped group, and at the ready to do whatever is needed at a small local theater. She loves to cook, bake, travel, read and mostly, talk to old friends and meet new people.